BRUISES

BRUISES

ANKE DE VRIES

translated by
STACEY KNECHT

FRONT STREET & LEMNISCAAT
Asheville, North Carolina

Originally published in the Netherlands under the title *Blauwe plekken*

Printed in the United States of America
First Front Street paperback edition, 2003

Library of Congress Cataloging-in-Publication Data
Vries, Anke de, 1936-
[Blauwe plekken. English]
Bruises / Anke de Vries : translated by Stacey Knecht.
—1st American ed.
p. cm.
Summary: While living in Holland, Michael meets Judith,
who is frightened, bullied, and beaten by her mother
and blames herself for the abuse she is enduring.
ISBN 1-886910-09-X (pb)
[1.Child abuse—Fiction. 1. Netherlands—Fiction.] I. Knecht, Stacey. II. Title
PZ7.V986Br 1995
[Fic]—dc20 95-40614

BRUISES

ONE

THERE WAS TROUBLE AHEAD. JUDITH COULD TELL BY THE WAY the front door banged shut, by the footsteps on the stairs.

Her body tensed, her eyes darted around the room. Was everything in its place? Nothing that might attract attention? Because that's what mattered most: that nothing attract attention. Least of all herself.

Her little brother Dennis was building a tower out of blocks. He was so absorbed in his game, he didn't even hear the footsteps. Or maybe it was the music ... the radio! Judith jumped out of her chair and nervously began turning the knob.

Too late! Her mother was standing in the doorway, still wearing her coat.

"Mommy, Mommy!" Dennis forgot all about his blocks and went rushing toward her, his arms outstretched.

Her mother's expression changed, as it always did when she looked at Dennis. She picked him up and hugged him tight.

"Now that's what I call a warm welcome, sweetie pie," she said.

Dennis wrapped his arms around her neck and covered her with kisses.

"Hello, Mommy," Judith mumbled. She stood there watching, her arms hanging limply at her sides. She saw how Dennis pulled the combs out of her mother's hair and stuck them in his own dark curls.

"Me pretty," he laughed.

"You silly thing, give them back." But Dennis wriggled free and ran off into the kitchen, clutching his treasures.

"Me Mommy's combs!" he shrieked with delight.

Without the combs, Mommy's hair hung in lank strands along her cheeks; blond, like Judith's. She went to the chest of drawers and rummaged around for a rubber band.

"What are you staring at?" she snarled at Judith. "Haven't you got anything better to do?"

Judith quickly sat back down at the table. How stupid of her to stand around like that! She bent over her notebook and got back to work on the essay that was due the following day. "An Afternoon Off," she'd called it. She already had half a page, but suddenly her mind went blank and she couldn't think of anything else to write.

Her mother pulled off her coat and flung it onto a chair. If *she* were ever to do a thing like that ...

"You must think I'm some kind of idiot, don't you? You think I didn't know the radio was on?"

Judith's heart began to pound. She'd been hoping her mother hadn't noticed. What should she do? Keep her mouth shut, or speak up? Whatever she did, it would be wrong. Dennis had been fiddling with the dial, and one of the stations was playing such a cheerful song that she hadn't wanted to switch it off. After that she'd started working on her essay and had forgotten all about the radio.

"Answer me!"

"Dennis ..." stammered Judith. "Dennis was turning the dial and ..."

"You know what's so disgusting about you?" Her mother's voice seemed to cut right through her. "The way you always blame that poor little boy. You know damn well I don't want the radio on. We'll get in trouble with the neighbors."

"It wasn't on loud. Really."

"Are you contradicting me?" She started coming toward her. Judith cringed and covered her head with her arms, but nothing happened. She waited anxiously.

"I can't trust you for a minute, can I?" her mother yelled. "Always sneaking around behind my back. You make me sick!"

She disappeared into the kitchen; it was almost as if she were trying to escape. Judith heard water running. She knew what her mother was doing: holding her wrists under the faucet and splashing water on her face.

Dennis scampered back into the room. "Play, play ..." he whined, tugging at Judith's sweater.

Slowly she got to her feet. Strange, the way her arms and

legs always felt like lead when Mommy was in one of her moods. How long would it last this time? When would Mommy come out again? What would she do? Judith could never be sure. The waiting was often the worst part.

This time, though, things went differently: her mother stayed in the kitchen. She'd taken the radio in with her and was listening to the news. But not for long; she soon switched over to a different station, one that played music. Loud music. The radio was on much louder than it had been that afternoon.

Judith shut her notebook; she'd finish her essay after supper. No use trying to get it done now. First she'd clear away Dennis's toys and give him a bath.

She picked all his things up off the floor and put them in the toy box. Dennis didn't make a fuss, thank goodness. He even tried to help her.

When they were done, Judith took him into the bathroom and filled the tub with water. Dennis placed his rubber duck on the edge and started getting undressed. His chubby fingers fumbled with the buttons on his shirt. Too hard. Okay, he'd try the shoes, that was easier. The moment Judith had her back turned, he threw one of his shoes in the tub.

"Shoe swim!" he announced triumphantly.

"Oh, Dennis, what did you do that for!" cried Judith as she fished the shoe out of the water.

"Shoe duck, too," Dennis said, beaming.

He looked so pleased that Judith had to laugh. Sometimes you just couldn't be angry with him.

Suddenly Judith saw her mother standing in the doorway. She hadn't heard her coming, because the water was running. Too late to hide the dripping shoe; Mommy had already seen it. Furious, she grabbed the shoe out of Judith's hands.

"You did that on purpose, didn't you? To spite me! How dare you? His brand new-shoes!" She dragged Judith out of the bathroom and gave her a shaking.

"No, Mommy ..." Judith's voice was small and forlorn. "Really, I—"

The first blow to her cheek made her gasp. Then came a

dry *whack* on the other cheek. Judith tried desperately to dodge the blows that followed.

"Don't, Mommy," she begged, "don't ..."

Her mother yanked at her hair. She mustn't scream, no matter what. That would only make her mother angrier.

"You drive me crazy!" By now it was raining blows and punches. Judith felt something warm trickling down her lips. Her head nodded back and forth.

She opened her mouth to scream, but nothing came out. Iron fingers squeezed her throat, stifling her cries. She was choking, choking, and all she could do was make strange gargling sounds.

"Mommy, Mommy ..." The thin little voice seemed to come from far away. The fingers let go; Judith went crashing to the floor and lay there, gasping for breath. Her mother towered over her, huge and threatening; she looked tall enough to reach the ceiling.

Dennis appeared. His eyes were wide with fear.

"Mommy mad?" His lip quivered.

Something changed in Mommy's expression. She stooped down and pressed him to her. Dennis kicked his legs wildly, struggling to get free.

All of a sudden she let him go, and ran into the kitchen.

Judith picked herself up and staggered back into the bathroom. Her hands trembled as she wiped away the blood that was dripping from her nose. She hoped her nose wouldn't swell up too much, because then she'd have to stay home from school again. She tried to stop the bleeding with cold water. When she tipped her head back, her neck ached.

"Judith ow?" Dennis asked shyly.

"No ... no."

Her voice sounded strangely hoarse, like the voice of a different person. I even look like a different person, she suddenly realized when she saw herself in the mirror.

She slowly undressed Dennis and lifted him into the tub. He sat very quietly and didn't squirm when she tried to wash him. He didn't even play with his duck.

"Judith, sweetie pie," he said gravely.

Judith laughed through her tears. She had an odd, crooked smile on her face.

"Judith, sweetie pie," Dennis repeated. He flung his wet arms around her neck and kissed her on the nose. She was just barely able to suppress a cry of pain.

TWO

JUDITH LISTENED TO THE RAIN PATTERING ON THE ROOF. SHE shivered; it was cold and damp in her attic room. Yet her cheeks burned as if she had a fever.

She ran her fingers over her face. Her nose wasn't too bad; with a bit of luck, you wouldn't be able to see a thing by morning. But the welts in her neck would take longer to heal.

And tomorrow she had gym ... She'd have to think up another excuse, just like the last time when she'd had so many bruises. Good thing she hadn't been at this school very long. Maybe no one would notice. She didn't like lying to her teacher, though; he was such a nice man.

Suddenly Judith remembered her unfinished essay. On top of everything else! And the notebook was still downstairs.

Judith rolled over. She was relieved to be lying in bed.

Supper had passed in silence. Only Dennis had said a few words now and then, in his own funny language, and looked searchingly at his mother; he, too, knew that something was wrong. Judith had hardly been able to swallow a bite, but she didn't dare refuse, for fear of another outburst.

After supper she'd put Dennis to bed, then quickly retreated to her own room.

Later that night, when her mother came upstairs, she'd lain in bed without moving a muscle. The door opened quietly; she heard footsteps in her room, which stopped when they reached her bedside. A voice whispered, "Are you awake?"

She kept her eyes closed and pretended to be asleep, but it wasn't easy when her heart was beating like a drum. What a relief it was when the footsteps finally headed toward the door!

Judith could never understand why Mommy came up to her room after she'd given her such a beating. Maybe it was to make sure she was still alive; once Mommy saw that she was still breathing, she always went out again.

She also could never understand why Mommy beat only her, and not Dennis. She really did do her best to help out, but it was never good enough. And usually things went wrong because she was so tense, but then Mommy always said she'd done it on purpose. To spite her. As if she didn't have enough trouble as it was.

Judith had heard it so many times before ... How hard it was bringing up two kids on your own, nobody to lean on. Her first husband was a bum. She was glad to be rid of him, the guy made her sick, but why did he have to saddle her with a baby? Then there was Uncle Ben, Dennis's father. A regular Prince Charming, but when you really needed him, forget it! Okay, there was the occasional handout for Dennis, but never enough, because he was already living with somebody else, who spent most of it on herself. "That woman is smarter than I am," Mommy would say scornfully. "I've always been stupid enough to let them walk all over me ..."

Judith had never seen her father, not even a picture of him. Mommy had ripped them all up, as if she wanted to forget he ever existed. It's strange, Judith often thought, I don't even know if I look like him. But she didn't dare ask. Her mother did still have a few pictures of Uncle Ben. He was a nice guy; too bad he and Mommy had been fighting so much lately. He'd even stood up for her once, when her mother was beating her with a hairbrush. That was years ago, before Dennis was born.

She hadn't heard him come in. Mommy was beating her black and blue and Uncle Ben had grabbed Mommy and yelled, "What's wrong with you? You're gonna kill that kid!"

"Keep out of it!" Mommy had screamed, and then they got into a terrible fight.

"You're crazy, you know that?" Uncle Ben had shouted. "Completely out of your mind! You're always down on her, and she hasn't done a thing!"

"How would you know what she's done? You're never here!"

"What would I want to hang around here for? With you nagging and complaining all day long?"

Judith had fled from the room, and later Uncle Ben had gone up to see her and said, "You and I are going out tomorrow. Your Mom's just upset, she needs some time off."

He'd taken her to the zoo. She would never forget that day. Uncle Ben bought peanuts for the monkeys, and she was allowed to watch the giraffes for as long as she liked. She thought they were the most beautiful animals of all. Especially their eyes, so gentle and friendly. For her next birthday, Uncle Ben had even given her a picture book about giraffes. She still thumbed through it from time to time.

That afternoon at the zoo, Uncle Ben had asked Judith if her mother often hit her. It was a hard question. If she said yes, he and Mommy would probably have another fight. So she said no.

"Then where'd you get those bruises on your legs the other day?"

She felt her cheeks burning, and mumbled that she'd fallen down. And then, right in front of everyone, Uncle Ben had picked her up and hugged her. It was kind of embarrassing but also kind of nice.

"Mommy's really sweet," she said to him later, as they walked around the Reptile House. "You like her too, don't you?"

"Usually, but sometimes I wouldn't mind feeding her to one of those guys," he'd said, pointing to the crocodiles, who followed them silently with bulging eyes. Judith had laughed, shivering. Imagine feeding Mommy to the crocodiles ...

But Uncle Ben had gone away, just the same. One Thursday night, without any warning. They didn't even have a fight.

At first Mommy had been very worried, but then she was furious. In the days that followed, Judith couldn't do anything right, and her mother gave her hell. One night Mommy smacked her so hard, she fell and hit her head against a cabinet.

What happened next, she couldn't remember, only that she was lying on the sofa. Mommy was nervously trying to staunch the flow of blood from a wound on her head, and kept asking her how she was feeling. Judith wanted to tell her that everything was fine, but it wasn't, because she felt like throwing up. Her head throbbed, and the light hurt her eyes.

A doctor came, a different one from the time before. Mommy always had a different doctor; none of them was ever good enough.

They'd agreed beforehand what they were going to tell him: that she'd fallen down the stairs.

"Stairs?" she'd mumbled weakly. They were living in an apartment at the time, and there weren't any stairs, just an elevator.

"The stairs at your aunt's house."

"Which aunt?"

"Aunt Ria."

But Aunt Ria lives in Canada, thought Judith.

When the doctor arrived, her mother did the talking. In a daze, Judith let the stream of words glide past her; it all sounded as if it had actually happened.

She, Judith, had fallen down the stairs—one of those horrible, steep staircases. No, not here, at her aunt's house. And to make things worse, she'd hit her head against a cabinet at the foot of the stairs, in the hallway.

Her mother watched anxiously as the doctor examined her.

"It's nothing serious, is it, Doctor? Yes, she did throw up once, and she says she's still feeling ill. What? A concussion? Oh, my poor baby ..."

She stroked Judith's hair. Was Judith imagining it, or were there really tears in Mommy's eyes?

The doctor asked why they hadn't called in their own physician. Mommy had an answer for everything. They'd just moved here, that was why. But that was a lie.

"You're going to have to stay in bed for a few days, young lady," said the doctor. "You've had a bad fall." He took another look at the wound on her head.

"This'll heal in no time. Your mom did a very good job cleaning it. I couldn't have done better. But from now on, you watch out for those staircases. Okay?" he said kindly, giving her hand a little squeeze.

"Yes, Doctor," she whispered.

After that, Mommy was especially nice to her. She even

stayed home from work for a couple of days. One afternoon as Mommy sat at the table peeling an apple, Judith suddenly began to cry.

"What's the matter now?" her mother burst out.

Judith wanted to tell her how sweet she was, how very sweet, but all she could manage was an unintelligible stammer.

"It's never enough, is it?" snarled her mother. She flung the half-peeled apple on the floor and stormed out, slamming the door behind her.

From then on, things were as bad as ever.

"There's nothing wrong with you, Judith," her mother jeered. "You're perfectly able to get out of bed. I'm not planning to use up my whole vacation waiting on you."

Judith's mother also sent away everyone who came to see her. A few of her classmates dropped by, but Mommy wouldn't let them in. "It's too tiring," she told them.

Mr. Beekman, Judith's teacher, phoned twice to ask if he could visit, but even he didn't get the chance. "There's no point," her mother said. "She'll be back at school any day now."

Judith had done everything she could to please her mother. She'd gotten out of bed, even though she was still feeling dizzy and had a headache, a dull throbbing above her eyes.

The headaches had been coming back since then. Judith compared them with her mother's moods: they were equally unpredictable. They'd come on very suddenly. Her neck would grow painfully stiff, and she couldn't stand bright light. The pain wore her out; it was a great effort just to keep her mind on her lessons at school. Sometimes she could barely follow what was being said.

Still, the headaches were a good excuse not to take part in gym or swimming. And that way she could hide the bruises on her back and arms.

Judith rolled over on her other side and started worrying about her essay again. Should she go downstairs and get the notebook? Then she could finish her essay in bed. She sat up, wondering what to do. If she went down very quietly, she could tell by the streak of light under the living room door whether her mother was still awake.

She slipped out of bed and tiptoed into the hallway. The house was deadly silent; in the distance, she heard a car driving off, a dog barking.

Now the stairs. She knew exactly which steps creaked, and skipped those. When she reached the bottom she tiptoed to the door, hardly daring to breathe. No sliver of light; her mother had gone to bed.

She hesitated, then reached for the doorknob. Suddenly she drew back her hand. Someone was in there, sobbing. It was her mother, Judith realized. She sounded helpless and lost.

Judith stood on the stairs, unable to move. She forgot what she'd come down for, and it wasn't until the crying had stopped that she turned around and crept back up the stairs.

Trembling, she crawled under her quilt. Mommy must've been crying about her, because she always made her so unhappy—though she never knew why. If only I could be more like Dennis, she thought enviously. He never made Mommy mad.

It was raining harder now. She really should get up and put down a bucket where the ceiling always leaked.

Maybe she should ... yes, she should really ...

Judith sank away into a dreamless sleep.

Several hours later she woke with a start but didn't know why. The room was dark and still; outside, it had stopped raining.

She looked at her alarm clock: quarter to five.

Judith dived down under the quilt. Hey, what was that? Something damp! Had she left the window open? As she sat up, the truth slowly dawned on her. She'd wet her bed.

She lifted the quilt; there was a sourish smell. Her pajama bottoms were soaking wet.

She hurriedly switched on the lamp beside her bed, and her eyes filled with tears when she saw the large, dark stain on the sheet.

Mommy mustn't find out, or there'd be trouble.

Shivering, she stripped off her pajama bottoms. Then she checked the quilt. Only one small, damp spot, thank goodness, but the sheet was in much worse shape. Judith pulled it off. The big, dark stain on the mattress grinned up at her. What if she turned it over? No, not now. Her room was right above her mother's and Dennis's. If she made too much noise, Mommy would wake up.

She'd sleep on the floor; then the mattress could dry. She carefully spread out her quilt and wrapped herself up in it. The floor was hard and cold, but that was the least of her worries. How was she ever going to conceal this from her mother?

First thing in the morning, she'd turn over the mattress, and after school she'd wash her pajamas and the sheet at the laundromat around the corner. She didn't dare use her mother's washing machine; she wasn't even allowed to. Mommy always turned it on, and Judith had to take out the laundry and hang it up.

Judith looked at her alarm clock again. Quarter past five. Only a few more hours to go before daylight.

When she woke up, she couldn't figure out what she was doing on the floor. But one look at the mattress and it all came rushing back. She got up and looked out the window. It was a clear, sunny morning. Judith sighed. The turtleneck sweater she was planning to wear to hide the welts was going to be very conspicuous.

Downstairs, she could hear Dennis's tiny footsteps and Mommy's voice.

Now was her chance. She flipped over the mattress, then carefully covered it with her quilt. That way, everything would look normal. She hid her sheet and pajama bottoms in the closet.

She was dying to take a shower, but then there'd be all kinds of questions, since she usually showered in the evening.

Her neck still hurt, especially when she turned her head. There was no mirror in her room, but she could just imagine what the welts looked like.

She pulled on her jeans and got out the turtleneck sweater. She hoped that Diana, who sat next to her in class, wouldn't tease her about it.

Judith breathed a sigh of relief. Her mother didn't seem to notice anything unusual. In fact, she didn't seem to notice anything but Dennis, whom she was trying to feed. He always dawdled over breakfast, but Mommy never lost her patience with him; she simply took it into account, and got up half an hour earlier.

Judith studied her mother's face: there wasn't a trace of sadness. Had she really been crying last night? Mommy was wearing her usual morning expression: one eye on the clock, a worried wrinkle for Dennis, and no time for Judith.

She doesn't even know I exist, thought Judith.

"Would you ... would you write me a note?" Judith asked softly. "We've got gym today."

Usually when she tried to get Mommy's attention, her mother snapped at her. "Stop nagging me," she'd say, or, "Haven't you got anything better to do?"

But this time she said nothing. She got up and went to the chest of drawers where she kept her notepad.

Judith knew just what she was going to write:

"Judith can't take part in gym today, she has a bad headache."
Sincerely yours,
C. Van Gelder.

Without a word, she put the note down next to Judith's plate.

THREE

JUDITH PEDALED AS FAST AS SHE COULD; SHE WAS AFRAID TO be late for school. Every movement made her neck and shoulder ache, and the thick turtleneck sweater was itchy and warm. It was still winter, but the air was so mild, it felt more like spring.

"Hey, wait for me!" She heard Diana's breathless voice behind her.

Judith slowed down, and moments later Diana was riding beside her, on her shiny new bike. Diana herself seemed to shine all over, too, Judith thought: nylon jacket, gleaming white sneakers, glossy hair, even the braces on her teeth flashed when she laughed. Next to Diana, Judith felt dull. What's more, she always asked the most annoying questions.

"Aren't you dying in that sweater?"

There she goes again, thought Judith.

"I can't believe you'd wear a dumb sweater like that to school," squealed Diana when they got to the bicycle rack. "I'd never want to look like such a geek."

"You already do." It was Michael, who was just putting his bike in the rack, a little farther down. He grinned at her.

"You jerk," Diana snapped, turning bright red because she had a crush on him.

Michael had started school after summer vacation. He was older than the rest of the class; taller, too. Sometimes his voice broke, which made everybody laugh—including Michael. "Wrong octave," he'd squeak.

Michael had a problem. He'd told them about it the very first day.

"I'm dyslexic," he'd said. "That's why I'm bigger than all of you."

"What's that?" asked Eva.

"It means you grow faster," said Diana, who always thought she knew everything.

"I hate to tell you," said Michael, "but it just so happens you're wrong. Dyslexic means you're not very good at reading or writing. At first everybody thought I was stupid, but I'm not. No way. I've just got this kind of technical malfunction up here." Michael tapped on the side of his head.

"I once saw something about that on TV," Robert told the class. "There was this guy, he must've been forty or so, and he couldn't even write a letter!"

"He probably had the same thing I do," said Michael, "only much worse. I can talk about stuff, but I can't write it down. That's why I've been held back twice. It just so happens, I'm almost thirteen."

Thirteen ... Everyone gazed at him in awe.

"What's your favorite team, Ajax or Feyenoord?" asked Robert.

"AC Milan," said Michael.

Michael even gave a little talk on dyslexia in front of the class.

He started by asking the teacher to write the name of the school, Cloverleaf Elementary, on the blackboard. Then he erased it and tried to write it himself. It took him a long time. Michael explained what gave him the most trouble. "If you wanna know the truth," he said with a laugh, "I have trouble with everything! I can never remember what words look like. Or letters, either. For instance, I'm always writing *b* instead of *d*, or *u* instead of *n*. I just can't tell them apart. Sometimes I even write whole words backwards!"

Michael talked for a while, and everyone understood it, more or less. Even Karel, who usually needed things explained three times. He did have one question, though. A really stupid one.

"How come you learned how to talk, if you can hardly read?"

The class roared, but Michael stuck up for Karel.

"That question isn't as stupid as you think," he said. "Talking's no problem for me. I only have to hear something once, and it gets stored away up here." Michael tapped on his head again. "It just so happens," he added, "I can even speak English."

"Where did you learn that?" asked Diana.

"Where do you think? I used to live in America!"

That made a big impression, especially on Diana, who fell madly in love with him.

When Michael was finished, the teacher gave him an *A*.

"Why not an *A+*?" Michael wanted to know.

"Because it just so happens," replied Mr. Beekman, "that I never give more than an *A*."

"Sounds like a good reason to me," said Michael, and he shook the teacher's hand.

Judith tried to pay attention, but her mind kept wandering. When should she give her teacher the note? At recess, or just before gym class? She jumped when everyone shut their history books, and realized she'd missed half the lesson.

"Before we go on," said Mr. Beekman, "I'd like you all to hand in your essays." He walked from desk to desk, collecting the sheets of paper.

"I left mine home," said Robert. He was lying; he hadn't finished his essay. The teacher looked down at him.

"It's the second time this has happened," he said.

"Sorry, Mr. Beekman," Robert bowed his head, as meekly as possible. Actually, it was the third time; he was glad the teacher couldn't count.

"Did I say second? This is the *third* time!" Mr. Beekman sounded annoyed. "Go home and get it, right now."

Robert jerked up his head.

"Do I ... do I have to go all the way home?" he asked.

"You heard me."

Robert shuffled unhappily out of the classroom.

"Bet he hasn't even finished it," Diana snickered, just loud enough for everyone to hear.

"Your essay, Judith?" The teacher was standing at Judith's desk.

"I haven't finished it yet, Mr. Beekman." She felt her cheeks burning.

"Why not?"

"I ... I had one of those headaches," she murmured faintly.

"Okay, let's see what you've done so far."

Judith rummaged nervously through her schoolbag. Mr. Beekman waited. He looked at her bowed head, the straight blond hair that hid her face. She must be suffocating in that sweater, he suddenly thought. She glanced up at him, pale, a look of panic in her eyes. There was something so helpless about that child. He could never be angry with her.

"Karel ..." Mr. Beekman had left Judith's desk and was moving on to the next.

"Michael ..."

Michael handed over his essay, beaming with pride. "Two whole pages," he announced.

"Not bad," his teacher said, smiling.

Judith bent over her reading workbook. Thank goodness, Mr. Beekman hadn't said anything. Now all she had to worry about was the note ...

Recess. The whole class stumbled out into the yard. Everyone but Judith, who lingered behind.

"Let's go, Judith," her teacher urged.

"I ... I've got another note," she mumbled, placing it hurriedly on his desk.

Mr. Beekman read it. No gym for Judith. Again! He'd have to have a talk with her mother. These headaches of hers weren't normal.

The day was over. Judith walked to the bicycle rack. She felt relieved that everything had gone so well. While the other children were in gym class, she had been allowed to finish her essay. She'd tried so hard to do her best, it made her cheeks glow. And she was really pleased with the way it turned out. She hoped Mr. Beekman would be, too.

She'd started all over again and made up a kind of fairy tale. About a poor mother who wanted to buy a present for her little girl, even though she hardly had any money. They went into town together, and Anna—that was the daughter's name—was allowed to pick out anything she liked.

"I want to give you something really beautiful," said Anna's mother.

Anna knew how poor her mother was. She could think of loads of stuff she would've liked to have, but her mother would never be able to afford it. Anna thought very hard.

"Made up your mind?" asked her mother.

"I can't think of a thing," said Anna. "I've got everything I could possibly want."

"Everything?" her mother exclaimed. "But dear Anna, you have nothing. You have hardly any clothes, and no toys at all."

"But I have you," said Anna.

When Anna said that, her mother picked her up and whirled her around, right in the middle of the street.

"My darling Anna." She said lovingly, "My dearest, darling Anna." Everyone who saw them had to smile because they'd never seen a mother who loved her daughter so much.

And then they went off to have ice cream at Florencia's, because they had just enough money for that.

Judith was about to get on her bike when she noticed that something was wrong.

"What's up?" asked Michael.

"Oh, just one of my tires."

"No problem," said Michael. "I've got a bicycle pump."

He began pumping away at the tire but soon stopped.

"It's punctured," he announced cheerfully.

"Punctured?" Judith looked at him in alarm. Now she'd be late picking up Dennis at the daycare center.

"No problem, I'll fix it. Come on."

"Where are you going?"

"Home, where I've got all my repair stuff. Get on the back of my bike. I can steer with one hand and hold on to your bike with the other."

Judith was so surprised, she followed his orders without thinking.

"Ha, ha ... Michael's got a girlfriend!" Robert whooped. "Michael's got a girlfriend!"

Michael ignored him and kept on pedaling. Now and then he swerved dangerously, and Judith had to cling to his jacket. Soon they were riding down a bike path, where there was less traffic. When they reached an intersection, Michael got off.

"This part's too risky," he said. "We better walk the rest of the way."

Judith walked behind Michael, her eyes fixed on his faded jacket. She was still amazed; she couldn't understand why he had offered to fix her tire. In the few weeks that she'd been at Cloverleaf they'd hardly exchanged a word, and now she was going home with him, just like that.

"Mr. Beekman's cool, don't you think?" asked Michael, who was walking beside her now.

Judith was startled. "Huh?"

"I said, Mr. Beekman's cool!" Michael repeated impatiently.

"Oh ... yes."

Michael looked away for a moment. She sure wasn't very talkative. He was sorry he'd even offered to help her. He'd only done it because she reminded him of Steffie, the girl who had lived next door to him in America, whom he hadn't seen for five years. But Judith wasn't Steffie. And she'd better not expect him to fix everything for her from now on.

"Look out," he warned, grabbing her by the shoulder. Judith was so lost in thought, she had nearly walked into a parked car.

"Ow." It was out before she knew it.

"Did I hurt you?" Michael asked, surprised.

"No ... no," stammered Judith. "It's just that I ... I banged my shoulder yesterday."

"Sorry."

"That's okay," said Judith quickly.

"We have to turn right here. I live at number eighty-five."

It was a fairly quiet street—a few trees here and there, even a bench. Alongside Michael's house was a flagstone path that led to the backyard.

As soon as Michael opened the garden gate, two little boys came running toward him. They looked so much alike, you could hardly tell them apart.

"Michael, Michael, we want a ride!" They tugged at his

jacket sleeve, and one of them tried to climb onto the back of his bike.

"Later," Michael promised. "First I've got a tire to fix."

Before Judith could even ask them their names, the kitchen door swung open and a little girl came skipping out.

"Are there any more?" asked Judith.

"Nope," laughed Michael. "That's it."

Then a woman appeared. She had a deep voice, and her movements were slow and unhurried, as if she had all the time in the world. The commotion around her didn't seem to bother her in the least.

The woman walked up to Michael and gave him a kiss. Michael hugged her back. Then she turned to Judith. "I'm so glad Michael brought you along. Are you two in the same class?"

"Yes, ma'am," Judith answered softly, lowering her eyes. She never knew how to behave with adults; she was always afraid she might do something wrong.

"This is Judith," said Michael. "She's got a flat tire."

"Would you kids like something to drink?"

"I better fix the tire first," said Michael.

One of the little boys grabbed Judith's hand and pulled her inside. "You can see my train," he said with a friendly smile.

"*Our* train," corrected his twin brother, who followed him around like a shadow.

"And I can make my train crash, too. Then all the carts fall down," the other boy went on proudly.

"Not 'carts,' 'cars,'" his brother corrected him again. "You can't even talk right."

"I can too!"

Judith watched as he placed the train on the tracks and rode it around. His twin brother told Judith that his name was David and his brother's name was Frank, and that he could talk so well because he was the oldest.

"David's only a little bit the oldest. Only two minutes," Frank grumbled.

"Two minutes is a whole lot. This much." David spread his arms wide.

Minutes ... Judith had completely forgotten about the time. She glanced at the clock: nearly quarter past four. She was supposed to have picked Dennis up fifteen minutes ago! What should she do? She looked around helplessly.

"Something wrong?" asked the woman, who had just come back in.

"My little brother ... I have to pick him up from daycare every afternoon. Now I'll be late."

"Why don't you give them a call? The telephone is in the hallway. Do you know the number?"

"Yes, ma'am," Judith mumbled, and rushed out of the room.

In her nervousness she dialed the wrong number. Try again, try again, she thought.

Moments later she heard the familiar voice of Sophie, one of the young women who worked at the daycare center.

"It's ... it's Judith. I have a flat tire."

"A flat tire? Hey, that can happen to the best of us! Does that mean you'll be a little late?"

"Yes."

"No problem," said Sophie good-naturedly. "I'll keep that brother of yours busy. I've got plenty of chores to do around here anyway. What time do you think you'll be here?"

"I don't know. I'm at Michael's, a boy from my class. He's fixing my tire."

"Sounds like a great guy. Listen, take your time, we'll be fine. See you when I see you."

But her reassuring words didn't make Judith feel any better. If her mother ever found out she'd been late ... She raced out into the backyard.

"Is my tire ready yet?" she asked.

"Hey, it just so happens I'm not a magician," said Michael. He sounded offended.

"I have to get my brother from the daycare center."

"Can't your mother do that?"

"She works."

"So call them up and tell them you'll be late."

"I've already done that," said Judith anxiously.

"Then everything's fine, right?"

No, everything's *not* fine, thought Judith, but Michael can't possibly know that.

Michael glanced up at her. What was wrong? he wondered. She no longer seemed to be aware of her surroundings. Not even of the twins, who were chasing each other all over the yard. She looked so lost, it made him feel uncomfortable.

"Afraid you're gonna get it, huh?" The words just slipped out.

Judith stared at him as if she'd been caught redhanded. "Who ... who would do that?"

"Who do you think? Your father."

She sighed, and looked almost relieved. "I haven't got a father ... I mean, I do have one, but I've never seen him. My parents are divorced."

"Oh." All of a sudden Michael seemed solely interested in the tire. "I'll just pump this up," he said, turning the bike upside down.

David and Frank had stopped running and come over to watch.

"Michael can do anything," David told Judith proudly. "He even fixed Mommy's clock, right, Michael? And he taught me English. 'Cause Michael used to live in America. Did you used to live in America too?"

"No."

"Can we go with you?" asked Frank.

"Maybe some other time. But now I have to go pick up my brother."

"What's his name?" both boys asked at once.

"Dennis. He's two."

"That's really little," said David. "We're ten, all together."

Michael was finished pumping.

"Is it red-peppered?" asked Frank.

"Not 'red-peppered,' 'repaired,'" corrected David.

Judith laughed. "Pretty funny brothers you've got," she said to Michael.

"They're not my brothers, they're my cousins."

"Your cousins? Are you just here for a visit?"

"No, I live here." He sounded so glum that Judith didn't ask any more about it.

"Thanks for your help," she said quickly. "See you tomorrow."

"See you," mumbled Michael, and he wandered back into the house.

FOUR

MICHAEL WENT UP TO HIS ROOM AND STRETCHED OUT ON HIS bed. His cheerful mood was completely gone, but he didn't know why.

He folded his hands under his head and stared up at the sports posters on the wall. His room wasn't finished yet; neither was the rest of the house, for that matter, even though they'd already been living here six months. Lots of stuff was still packed away in boxes.

"It'll be just fine, you'll see," Aunt Elly had assured him. "If we need anything, all we have to do is open a box!"

Michael had to smile in spite of himself. With Aunt Elly, everything was always "just fine." She hardly ever made a fuss. Only if she felt it was really necessary. And then there was no stopping her, thought Michael, remembering how she'd dealt with his father.

It was more than three years now since he'd moved in with Aunt Elly and Uncle Bob. As far as David and Frank were concerned, he was their big brother.

Michael sighed. Why did he feel so lousy all of a sudden? Was it because of what he'd said to Judith?

"Afraid you're gonna get it?" he'd blurted out.

She'd given him the strangest look. Actually, she was a pretty strange girl, that Judith. Very quiet, very shy. A lot different from the other girls in his class. If she hadn't looked so much like Steffie, he'd probably never even have noticed her.

What had made him ask her that question? *He* hadn't ever been beaten by *his* father. If only he had; then he could've fought back. That is, if he'd had the nerve.

But he knew he'd never win.

His father was still in America. Michael only had to hear his voice over the phone, and he clammed up—a high, disapproving voice. A voice that never faltered. His father was smart; he worked as a lawyer for a big American company. If they were in trouble, he always got them out of it. Everything his father did was a success. Why couldn't Michael be proud of him? Why did he still frighten him, even after all these years?

Michael could clearly remember the day they'd left for America. His mother, Aunt Elly's sister, had died several months before. The whole house suddenly seemed quiet and empty.

Then Aunt Elly arrived. She was still in college at the time, and not yet married. She came to take care of him, but he ended up taking care of her, because she wasn't very good around the house. But she didn't seem to mind. She let him do all sorts of things, even cook supper, and they built a rabbit hutch together, with chicken wire across the front. Aunt Elly always made Michael feel big and important. They talked a lot about his mother, too, whom he no longer missed quite as much with Aunt Elly around.

Things were just getting back to normal when his father announced that they were moving to America. From that day on, his life changed completely.

Schiphol Airport. A cold and dreary afternoon. One hour to go. That's when Michael's father discovered the plastic bag he had hidden behind his back.

"What've you got there?"

"My bear," whispered Michael.

His father had told him, many times, that he was much too big for a teddy bear. Bears were for *little* boys. He looked down at him and asked, "How old are you, Michael?"

"Six."

"Is six big or little?"

He shrugged, but a vague feeling of uneasiness crept over him.

"I think six is big," said his father.

Michael was quite pleased to hear that, but then his father went on, "And big boys have to act big, don't they?"

He nodded.

"Big boys don't play with bears," said his father firmly. "This is a perfect opportunity to give him up, Michael. You and I are going to America, to start a new life. Just the two of us—*without* the bear. We can get along just fine on our own."

He stared at his father, speechless, the plastic bag with the one-eyed, one-eared bear clutched tightly against his chest.

"I understand. You want to throw the bear away all by yourself," said his father, pointing to a gray garbage bin.

Michael shook his head vehemently.

"Then I'll do it for you." He sounded slightly disappointed.

He was just reaching for the bear when Michael turned and ran. He pushed past the other passengers, raced blindly up a staircase, and shot into the first door he saw. Inside, women were combing their hair and washing their hands.

One of the women laughed at him, and said something in a language he didn't understand. Another asked, "What happened, did you lose your mommy?"

He didn't answer, just looked around, panting.

"I use Chanel Number Five," a woman was saying, and she took out a bottle and began spraying herself.

As the sweet scent tickled his nostrils, he heard his father's voice, "Michael ... Michael ..."

Without thinking, he hurled himself at the woman holding the bottle, clasping her desperately around the waist. The bottle slipped through her fingers and smashed against the floor. The smell was overwhelming.

"Look what you've done!" cried the woman. "That was my good perfume! What're you doing in the ladies' room anyway?" Indignant, angry eyes.

"Michael!" His father's voice, right outside the door.

The woman grabbed him by the shoulder and asked, "Are you Michael?"

She pushed him out in front of her into the corridor.

"Does he belong to you?" she demanded.

"Yes."

"Well, you'd better keep an eye on him in the future. He just broke my bottle of expensive perfume!"

"I'd be happy to reimburse you." His father reached for his wallet.

At first the woman refused the money, half-heartedly, and then accepted it. The three of them were enveloped in a nauseating cloud of perfume.

"He's probably just afraid of flying," she said, glancing at Michael. She sounded a bit friendlier now.

His father gave a quick nod, then took him by the arm and led him silently down the stairs. When they reached the bottom, he stopped; his hand was still firmly clasped around Michael's arm.

"From now on, I want no more of these childish games, Michael," he said in a calm, steady voice. "Is that clear?"

Michael nodded, his throat tight.

They walked through the departure hall. When they came to a garbage bin, his father stopped again.

"Well?"

Heart pounding, eyes blurred with tears, Michael threw in the plastic bag.

"Now you're really a big boy," said his father. The hand on his shoulder felt like lead.

In the plane he couldn't swallow a bite, no matter how much the stewardess urged him to eat.

"It's all the excitement," explained his father.

Then came the years in America.

For the first few months, Michael listened in amazement to the strange, nasal sounds, but it wasn't long before he, too, was speaking like a native. He even spoke English to his father.

He was sent to an American school. At first it was fun, but that soon changed. The letters of the alphabet, which had looked so harmless, became his greatest enemies. He was unable to read or write without making mistakes; he switched words around, left out letters, or wrote them upside down. Language became an indecipherable puzzle.

But the worst part of all was that his father assumed he was just being stubborn—and lazy.

"It's time we did something about this," he said, and made Michael come to his office after school to do his homework.

"I don't think I've ever met anyone as unwilling to learn as you are," said his father, looking at all his mistakes. "It's almost as though you're doing it on purpose."

"That's not true," said Michael despondently. "I swear, it's not true."

After a while he began stuttering. Whenever he had to read aloud in class, he'd struggle his way through the sentences while the other children snickered. His father always managed to keep his patience, despite Michael's stammering, but his stony silence only made Michael more nervous. Then he began getting sick: inexplicable rashes on his back and stomach, sudden high temperatures. Even when he had to stay in bed, his father gave him books to read and assignments to do; television, of course, was out of the question.

Once his father caught him watching a Lassie movie, and he was punished: he'd have to skip Peter's birthday party the following Sunday. Michael called his friend to say he couldn't come, but made the mistake of telling him he was being punished.

"Who's punishing you?"

"My father."

"Why? What did you do?" Peter asked curiously.

"I watched a movie, on TV."

"Late at night?"

"No, in the afternoon."

"Why would anybody get punished for that?" Peter exclaimed.

The next day the whole class knew. Michael made up some story about how, in Holland, children under the age of eight were never allowed to watch television. Everyone thought that was very sad. But Susan, a bright little girl with a ponytail, said he was lying. She had a Dutch cousin who was five years old and could watch as much TV as she liked.

"That's because she's a girl. It's different for girls," he said desperately, hoping to convince them. But it was no use. No one believed him anymore.

—

They moved four times. Each time, a new school, different children.

Then he met Steffie. She lived in the house next door, and had big gray eyes. Steffie talked a lot, and she was also really good at reading out loud. Sometimes she read him poetry, in her clear, high voice, and if there was a poem he liked he'd ask her, "Can you read it over?" After that, he knew the poem by heart. Steffie never understood how that was possible, and Michael understood it even less. He thought it had something to do with her voice.

Steffie shared everything with him. If she had a chocolate bar or a popsicle, she always gave him half.

"Why do you share stuff with me?" he asked her one day after she'd given him a handful of marbles.

"Sharing is fun," she said. "If you share, you both get something. Right?"

She'd looked at him questioningly with those big gray eyes.

"Watching TV alone is much less fun than watching with Mommy," she went on. "When we watch together I can laugh more, because Mommy laughs, too."

Michael nodded. He thought of his father. They never watched TV together; he wasn't even allowed to watch by himself.

As if she'd guessed his thoughts, Steffie asked, "Do you like your dad?"

"No," Michael answered. When he realized what he'd said, he felt guilty.

"Why not?" asked Steffie.

"He made me throw away my bear," said Michael. "That's why." He'd never told anyone about his bear before.

"What bear?"

"I only had one. His name was Doodle. When we moved to America, I wasn't allowed to take him with me. My father said I was too old to play with teddy bears."

"You're never too old for bears," Steffie said. "My father still has a lot of his toys. He's got five bears. They're really old, and he takes very good care of them. Sometimes we play with them, me and my dad, and he tells me all the things his bears used to do. One of them was always naughty, that was the polar bear. He never wanted to go to bed, and when it was his bedtime he always used to hide, and then my dad had to go looking for him." Steffie laughed.

Suddenly she stood up and ran into the house. "Don't go away!" She called out over her shoulder.

A few minutes later she was standing in front of him again, her hands behind her back.

"Close your eyes," she said, and he did.

She placed something soft in his hands.

"Okay, you can look."

He was holding a small bear: a koala bear from Australia, Steffie explained. "That's a really big country, with really little bears. He's my favorite bear, but you can have him since you don't have any of your own. I've got six more."

Michael was so happy, he didn't know what to say.

"You think he's sweet," said Steffie, who understood.

He nodded, and didn't know why he suddenly felt like crying. Steffie came up close and put her arms around him.

That was the best afternoon he'd ever had.

It was Steffie, too, who had stood up to his father. On a Sunday morning, when he was doing his spelling exercises.

There was someone at the door. His father got up and answered it.

"I'm here to play with Michael," Steffie announced.

"Another time, perhaps. Michael's busy."

"What's he doing?" asked Steffie.

"His homework."

"But it's Sunday!" cried Steffie. "You're not supposed to do homework on Sunday, you're supposed to play!"

"When Michael is finished, he'll come out and play." He shut the door.

An hour later, the doorbell rang again.

"Is Michael finished yet?" asked Steffie.

"No."

"How much longer will it take?"

"That depends on Michael. If he works hard, he'll be finished very soon."

When she rang the bell for the third time, his father told her she'd have to stop.

"I want to play with Michael."

"Michael has to work."

"But it's *Sunday,*" Steffie protested.

His father was about to shut the door again when Steffie cried out, "I think you're a really stupid man!"

There was a brief silence. Michael held his breath.

"And I think you're a very rude little girl," replied his father.

He didn't say a word about it when he came back in, though he must've known that Michael had heard them.

It wasn't until late in the afternoon that Michael was given permission to go outside.

He ran to Steffie's house and rang the bell, but nobody answered. He walked around the back and found a note Steffie had taped to the kitchen door. In her large, round handwriting were the words "I WENT OUT WITH MOMMY AND DADDY."

Disappointed, he trudged back home. That night, when he went to bed, his father told him they were moving again—this time, to Washington.

His last year in America ... Even now, when he thought back to that time, he was overcome by a feeling of powerlessness.

Without Steffie, he'd been lonelier than ever. At school, things got worse every day, and when he stuttered, the other kids laughed right in his face. There's something wrong with me, he thought, maybe I haven't got any brains, or not enough. That must be it, because everyone else can read and write, except me.

He also began having the strangest dreams. About his mother, whom he could only vaguely remember. In his dreams he'd go looking for her, wandering endlessly through empty rooms, opening doors that led him into other empty rooms. But he could never find her. His legs moved more and more slowly, the air grew so dense he could hardly breathe, and behind every door was that desolate emptiness.

Some nights he didn't dare fall asleep because he was so afraid he might have one of those disturbing dreams, from which he'd wake up bathed in sweat.

Michael's father was working harder than ever, and his patience began to wear thin. But it wasn't his father's impatience that Michael feared; it was his unspoken contempt. When Michael brought home his report card, his father signed it without a word, but Michael could hear his disapproval—even in the scratching of the pen.

One day, after Michael had gotten yet another bad grade, he couldn't face his father, and he ran away. He wandered for hours through unfamiliar streets and parks, and when evening came he found a garage that somebody had left unlocked. There was a car inside. He crawled into the back seat and immediately fell into a deep, dreamless sleep. He slept until morning, when he was awakened by the sound of a woman's voice.

"Hey, looks like I've got company."

Michael scrambled out of the car and tried to escape, but she grabbed his arm.

"Wait, it's okay. Who are you?" the woman asked. He shrugged, as if he didn't know.

"Maybe you'll remember after a nice breakfast," she said heartily. "Come on inside." She held out her hand, which felt strong and firm, and led him into her kitchen.

"What would you rather have, toast or cornflakes?"

"Toast."

He was suddenly starving, and the smell of toast made his stomach clench like a fist.

"Sit down," said the woman. "Here's a glass of milk while you're waiting."

The little kitchen was cozy and warm, and outside, in the garden, was a tree full of apples.

"Do you have to pick those all by yourself?" he asked, pointing to the tree.

"The apples? Yes, it's quite a job," she said as she squeezed a few oranges.

"What do you do with them?"

"I give most of them to the neighbors. They use them for apple pie."

The woman—she wasn't young and she wasn't old—put his breakfast on the table and then sat down opposite him.

"Taste good?"

He nodded.

"Do you remember your name yet?"

"Michael." He pronounced it the Dutch way; he didn't say "Mike," which was what they called him at school.

"I'm Helen. Where are you from?"

"Holland."

"And where do you live now?"

He stared down at his plate. If he told her, it was all over.

"I'll bet you ran away," said Helen.

He nodded.

"Why?"

"Because I'm stupid."

"What makes you think that?"

She leaned on her elbows and looked at him kindly. Her eyes were pale green with tiny gold flecks.

"I got another bad grade. I always get bad grades," he admitted gravely.

Now her expression would change, a wrinkle of disapproval would appear around her mouth. But no—it didn't seem to faze her, not in the least.

"Which subjects do you get bad grades in?"

"Almost everything."

"Gym, too?"

"No, not gym. But gym doesn't count. It's not important."

"Who says?"

"My father."

There was a silence. "And your mother? What does she say?"

"I haven't got a mother."

"Oh." Another silence. "And you? Do you think gym is important?"

"Me? Yeah. Gym's great. Especially swimming."

"Well, that's a relief." The woman sighed and looked pleased. "I happen to be a gym teacher," she said, "and I don't think you're at all stupid. In fact, I think you're very smart. And resourceful."

Was she making fun of him? No, she wasn't; he could tell by the look on her face. She asked him how old he was.

"Eight."

And then she told him she'd never met an eight-year-old boy who had run away from home and was smart enough to find a garage to sleep in.

"I think you've got a really good head on your shoulders. Imagine being able to find a safe place to sleep, under such difficult circumstances. I mean, nobody runs away just for the fun of it."

She took an apple out of the fruit bowl, and bit in. "Did you run away from home all because of a bad grade?"

He nodded. He couldn't possibly explain to her what that meant.

"Your father's going to be worried."

He hadn't even thought of that! Maybe he'd be *glad* that Michael was finally gone. But as it turned out, his father had been very worried. He'd even notified the police, who had spent hours searching for Michael. When Helen phoned him he came right away and seemed relieved.

"Your son's a smart kid," Helen had told him as they were leaving. "And he loves gym, especially swimming."

Michael still didn't know if his father had heard her.

From then on, a girl came to their house every day to take care of him. Her name was Sally. She'd sit on the phone for hours, and she always invited her boyfriend over, which Michael wasn't supposed to tell his father. In exchange, he was allowed to watch TV.

One evening his father came home early. Sally was fired on the spot.

Then Aunt Elly and Uncle Bob came to stay, with the twins, and that visit had changed everything.

Aunt Elly and his father spent the whole time arguing.

One night he heard her shouting: "Are you blind?! Can't you see what you're doing to that poor kid?"

Endless discussions followed, and one day his father gave him a choice: either he could stay in America, or he could go back to Holland with Aunt Elly and Uncle Bob.

He didn't have to think twice.

So much had happened in the past three years. Michael was no longer afraid to go to school. He now knew the reason for his "stupidity," that it was something he could do nothing about. He was given tutoring, and even began stuttering less.

Michael knew, too, that Aunt Elly and Uncle Bob loved him just the way he was. They signed him up for a swimming club and let him join the basketball team. Aunt Elly never put him down; she encouraged him in everything he did, and made him feel like part of the family.

Michael's thoughts were interrupted by the twins, who came tearing up the stairs and burst into his room.

"You gotta come set the table!" they cried.

Michael sat up. "Why do *I* always have to do that?" he moaned.

"Because you're big," said David. "That's why."

"Little kids have it easy," Michael mumbled. He rolled out of bed and followed them down the stairs.

FIVE

JUDITH ARRIVED AT THE DAYCARE CENTER ALL OUT OF BREATH.

"You didn't have to rush," said Sophie, shaking her head when she saw Judith's flushed cheeks.

"Was ... was Dennis any trouble?" Judith panted.

"Not a bit. He had fun, didn't you, Dennis? I did my chores, and he followed me around with a dustcloth. He's a great little helper!"

Dennis was busy dusting a chair and didn't seem to have any intention of going with Judith. "Stay with Sophie," he said firmly.

"See what I mean? We're buddies," Sophie said playfully. "Would you like something to drink?"

"Yes, please." Judith felt better, now that she saw that everything was all right with Dennis.

Sophie handed her a glass of Coke. She drank it down in one gulp.

"Boy, that was fast," said Sophie.

"I was pretty thirsty."

"Want some more?"

Judith nodded shyly.

"You come here every day to pick up your brother," said Sophie, refilling her glass. "I don't think you've ever been late. But does that leave you enough time for yourself?"

"Oh, sure," Judith lied. Time for myself, just think ... When she got home with Dennis there were always loads of things to be done, since Mommy worked all day.

"When?"

"Oh, you know ... on the weekend. I usually go play with my friend. Or she comes to play with me."

"That's nice," said Sophie. "What's her name?"

"Diana."

Judith could just imagine it! Diana at her house, or she at Diana's. It had never happened. She wouldn't have the nerve to ask her mother if she could bring someone home from school.

"And Michael?"

"I haven't known Michael that long." Judith was glad she didn't have to lie anymore. "He saw I had a flat tire, and he fixed it for me."

"Men who fix flat tires are worth having around." Sophie grinned. "That's how I met my boyfriend. One night, about a year ago, some jerk slashed my tires. I was furious! I still had a long way to go, and it was a pretty deserted road. Not one streetlight! Really creepy. Suddenly this guy appears on his bike and asks, 'Trouble?' I could tell by his voice that he wasn't some kind of weirdo.

"So I said, 'Yeah. Somebody's wrecked my tires. Both of them.' '*Double* trouble,' he said. 'I can give you a lift, if you don't mind sitting on the back of this wobbly old thing.' 'Anything's better than *this*,' I said, and that's how it all began. He fixed my tires, and we've been living together ever since!"

Sophie was so friendly that Judith felt more and more at ease.

"Listen, Judith," she went on as she helped Dennis into his coat, "if you ever feel like going home after school with one of your friends, just say so, okay? I'll take care of Dennis. I always have plenty to do around here anyway. Believe me, I know what's it like to have to pitch in around the house. I come from a big family—six kids!—and I was the oldest girl, so you can imagine how busy I was. You remind me of myself when I was younger, always doing what I was told, no time for myself. So don't forget, if you need me, let me know."

Judith blushed.

Laughing, Sophie grabbed her by the shoulders and gave her a playful shake. "Promise?"

"Ow!" Once again it just slipped out.

"Hey, I didn't hurt you, did I?" Sophie asked, surprised.

"I banged my shoulder yesterday," Judith told her. "It's still sore."

"Let me have a look. Maybe you did something to your collarbone."

"No ... no ..." said Judith hurriedly, "it'll go away by itself. I really have to leave now."

"Will you remember what I said?"

Judith nodded. "You won't tell my mother, will you?" She asked suddenly. "About the flat tire, and that I got here too late?" She looked anxiously at Sophie.

"Of course not," said Sophie. "That's between you and me."

She saw the relieved expression on Judith's face.

Sophie walked them to the front door, then stood in the doorway for a while, watching them go.

What was that all about? she wondered. Why didn't Judith want her mother to know she'd had a flat tire?

Judith walked her bike down the street, laughing and joking with Dennis, who was sitting on the back. What a wonderful day it had been! No problems with Mr. Beekman about the essay, and then Michael fixing her tire, and now Sophie. She felt like singing.

Even when she got home, that lighthearted feeling stayed with her—until she suddenly remembered the night before. It was too late to take her sheet to the laundromat; she'd have to do it the next day. But now that she was alone she could get clean sheets out of the closet, and her mother would never notice.

Judith quickly made her bed, then sat down to do her homework.

Where was Mommy? Judith kept looking up at the clock: it was almost nine-thirty. She'd finally gotten Dennis to bed; he could be so impossible sometimes! Fortunately, there had been leftovers in the fridge from the night before, which she'd warmed up for him. She herself hadn't eaten yet.

Could something have happened to her mother? Judith went to the window and looked up and down the street. No sign of the car. She was getting hungry. Maybe she should eat ...

Standing at the counter, she made herself a peanut butter sandwich—not her favorite, but there was nothing else in the house. Just as she was sitting down to eat, she heard a door slam in the foyer and voices on the stairs.

Judith ran into the hallway and saw her mother stumbling up the stairs, followed by a man in a light raincoat. Her cheeks were red, and she looked dazed. Every so often she caught hold of the banister and swayed back and forth.

"Hey, didn't you tell me you had a son?" asked the man. "We must've drunk more than I thought, 'cause I could swear that's a girl up there."

Her mother started giggling. "It *is* a girl. I've got a daughter, too."

By this time she'd reached the top of the stairs and was struggling to get out of her coat.

"Lemme give you a hand with that, baby," the man said, grinning. "I'm a lot better at taking clothes off than putting them on."

"Watch your language, will you? We're not alone!" her mother burst out. She teetered into the living room.

"Oooh, the lady's got a temper," the man teased. He followed her into the living room and closed the door behind him. Judith heard stifled laughter. A few minutes later, her mother came back out. She tried to speak normally but kept stumbling over her words.

"You should ... you shouldn't be up this late," she slurred. "Whatsa ... How's Dennis?"

"I gave him supper and a bath, and put him to bed."

"Good girl," her mother mumbled. "C'mon now ... you go to bed too."

Judith wanted to tell her that she'd been waiting up for her, and that all she'd eaten was a sandwich, but her mother had disappeared into the living room again.

She heard her mother laughing. It sounded forced, unnatural. Or did it only seem that way to Judith because her mother hardly ever laughed?

That same evening, Judith's teacher was going over his pupils' essays. "Could you do me a favor?" he asked his wife, who had just come in with a cup of coffee.

"I already have," she said, putting the coffee down in front of him.

He laughed. "Okay, another favor. Would you have a look at this essay?"

"Why? Have you discovered some 'child wonder'?"

"No, far from it! I'm just curious to hear what you think." He handed his wife a sheet of paper.

"Judith Van Gelder," she read aloud. The handwriting was cramped and uneven, and many of the letters were disconnected.

"An Afternoon Off" was the title of the essay. She sat down and began to read.

"What do you think?" her husband asked after a while.

"It's touching," said his wife, pensively. "She writes all about the ideal mother. The kind of mother every child would love to have. What's her own mother like?"

"No idea. The only contact I've had with her so far has been through notes. And they're always the same, about how her daughter has a headache and can't take part in gym. Judith hasn't been in my class all that long, only about six weeks."

"Is she a good student?"

"No. She was held back a year, so she's somewhat older than the rest of the children. But she looks younger. She strikes me as a fairly troubled little girl, and she doesn't tend to mix with the other children."

"If I were you, Arno, I'd keep an eye on her."

"Why do you say that?"

His wife shrugged, and peered back down at the spikey letters on the page.

"I don't know ... But you're obviously worried about her too. Otherwise you wouldn't have asked me to read this."

"You know me too well," he said, smiling, as she handed him back the essay.

"You wanna hear something weird?" Sophie said that night to her boyfriend Richard.

But he wasn't listening; he had his eyes glued to the television screen, where soccer players were running around on a bright green playing field.

"Anybody home?" she teased.

"Huh? What is it?" Richard looked up, annoyed.

"Wanna hear something weird?"

"I'll tell you what *I* think is weird. That you never leave me alone when there's a really good match on TV. Why can't it wait?"

"Why can't you watch and talk at the same time?" Sophie complained. "They aren't going to play any better just because we keep our mouths shut."

"I'm trying to concentrate. Look, a goal!" cried Richard. "Damn, just missed it!"

"Don't worry, pal, they'll replay that goal at least fifty times. You and your soccer." Sighing, Sophie got out the iron and ironing board.

Richard didn't hear her; he was staring at the screen again. The goal was shown over and over, from various angles.

"Okay, so what's so weird?" he asked a few minutes later, his eyes still on the screen.

"That you don't just go watch that stupid game at your parents' house," said Sophie crossly. "And while you're at it, maybe you could get your mother to iron your shirts."

Richard grinned. "I couldn't bear to be away from you, Soph. You know that. I'd even miss that nagging of yours. Now, would you please tell me what you think is so weird?"

"Somebody having a flat tire and being too scared to tell her mother."

"Unless it was her mother's bike and she wasn't supposed to be riding it."

"No, it was her own bike."

"Then that somebody has a pretty nasty mother."

"No, that's not it either. I know her. She brings her son to the daycare center every morning. If anything, she's *too* concerned."

"In other words, a bundle of nerves," said Richard, casting a sidelong glance at the screen. A group of players were kicking the ball around the midfield.

"What do you mean?"

"A bundle of nerves, probably divorced. Drops her precious son at the daycare center and rushes off to a boring job with a boss who drives her crazy ... and her daughter has to pay, because Mom's gotta take it out on somebody. I bet she beats the hell out of that kid."

"Richard, can't you be serious for a change?" Sophie burst out. She glared down at the T-shirt she was ironing.

"I *am* being serious. Hey, did you see that pass? Now that jerk's going to miss! What'd I tell you? The guy should've stayed home!"

"What makes you think her mother beats her?" Sophie asked after the referee had blown the whistle at the end of the first half.

"What makes me think that? Because I had this friend once whose father used to clobber him whenever he was in the mood. Nobody knew about it except me, but I had to swear not to tell, because if anyone found out, his father would beat him to death. That's what he told me. On his tenth birthday he got a bike. He was only allowed to ride it on Sundays, never during the week. One time he did anyway, and he rode over a nail. Great big hole in his tire. You should've seen his face ... I can't describe it. So I offered to tell his father that it was me who'd taken the bike out of the cellar and ridden it over the nail. I felt like a real saint, making that offer, and I went through with it, too, even though I was scared out of my mind, 'cause his father had this deadpan expression and eyes like granite. And I knew the guy was a heavy drinker, which didn't make it any easier. Everything was going fine, until my friend's little brother came in and told his father the real story. What went on that night, I don't know, but the next morning he was dead—my friend, I mean. If you ask me, he jumped out the window. He lived seven floors up. The papers said he was probably sleepwalking, that he fell out the window in his sleep. Do you believe that? I sure don't."

"My God," Sophie gasped.

"You can say that again." Richard sat there for a while,

staring into space. "Frank—that was his name. At school we all used to call him Frankie, Frankie Wieringa, because he was such a scrawny little kid. He had a good voice, though, I can remember that. Kind of high, like a girl's, really unusual ... but what good did it do him?"

Richard fell silent. The players filed back out onto the field, and the second half began.

Sophie unplugged the iron and snuggled up next to Richard on the sofa. He put his arm around her.

"I didn't know you were a soccer fan," he said.

"Neither did I," said Sophie. "Just goes to show you how people can change."

SIX

JUDITH'S MOTHER CAME OUT OF THE BEDROOM, YAWNING. She rubbed her eyes, which were slightly swollen.

"I'm not going in to work today, I'm too hung over," she said as she shuffled into the kitchen. "You bring Dennis to the daycare center."

Judith looked up at the clock and panicked. If she brought Dennis now she'd be late for school, but she didn't dare refuse.

She quickly began feeding her little brother. Her mother had made oatmeal, but Dennis didn't feel like eating; every time the spoon came too close, he turned his head away and clamped his mouth shut.

"I ... I'm afraid I'll be late for school—" Judith began carefully.

"Doesn't matter, just this once." Her mother gave another huge yawn and tried to get Dennis to eat, but it didn't do much good.

In the meantime, she started telling Judith all about the night before. How she'd gone out for a drink after work with one of the other women from the office. In the bar she'd met Nico, and they'd hit it off immediately.

Strange ... whenever Mommy had just met a man she liked, she always seemed different. She'd start confiding in her, as if she were one of her girlfriends.

"He sells insurance," she explained. "Come on, Dennis, no more dawdling, sweetie pie, let's see if you can eat this whole bowl. So anyway," she continued, "Nico took me out for dinner. We had such a great time! We just talked and talked, kept ordering more wine, and before we knew it, it was nine o'clock. You weren't worried, were you?"

"A little," Judith admitted.

"You didn't have to be. I knew you could manage with Dennis. I even said that to Nico. I said, 'No problem, my daughter'll take care of everything.'"

Judith was pleased with the compliment, although she

knew it was a lie. Nico himself had said that her mother hadn't even told him she had a daughter!

"He promised to call today. Think he will?"

"Sure." Judith really hoped he would, too, because if he didn't, her mother would be in a rotten mood.

"And Wilma, my friend from work? Boy, was she jealous. You remember Wilma, the one with the curly hair—I'm sure you've met her before. Well, she was absolutely green, because he asked me out and not her. You just wait, she won't look at me for a week!" Her mother snickered triumphantly, shaking back her long blond hair.

Judith said nothing. She had met Wilma once, a woman with a broad face and deep-set eyes, which had something wary about them.

"So, you're Judith," she'd said, looking her up and down.

She'd nodded.

"What's the matter, you lost your tongue?" her mother had snapped.

"Hello, ma'am," she'd mumbled quickly.

As she was going up to her room she'd heard her mother saying, "You never know what to expect from that girl. She can really get under your skin."

Judith had often thought about that last remark. What was it she did wrong, and how was she supposed to behave to win her mother's approval?

"Wilma's jealous," her mother continued, "because Nico fell for me, and not her. She can't stand that. Come on, Dennis, just a few more bites. That's my big boy." She wiped his mouth and gave him a hug. Judith watched in silence.

"Hey, don't just stand around daydreaming. Make yourself useful for a change. Go get Dennis's jacket."

When Judith returned with the jacket, her mother said, "I'll pick Dennis up this afternoon. You don't have to bother."

Judith cast one last glance at the clock. She was going to be at least fifteen minutes late.

Judith lifted Dennis onto the back of her bike and started

walking down the street. She didn't dare ride because she was afraid he might fall off.

As she passed the first-floor window, she saw the curtains move and felt Mrs. Van Klaveren's eyes on her back. "The Snoops," her mother always called the elderly couple.

"There they go," Mrs. Van Klaveren informed her husband.

"Who?" he asked, even though he already knew the answer.

"That girl from upstairs, and her little brother."

"The mother, too?"

"No."

Mrs. Van Klaveren had rheumatism, and spent the whole day sitting in a chair by the window. Her husband took care of her and did the shopping. Once a week, they had a young woman in to help, Tilly. "She's all thumbs," Mrs. Van Klaveren had complained one evening. "At least she's got a friendly smile," said her husband. "Who cares about that?" Mrs. Van Klaveren replied sharply. "I could do with a little less smiling and a lot more cleaning!"

But his wife's grumbling no longer bothered him; he'd grown so used to it, he hardly even heard it anymore.

"That girl's mother came home with a man last night," his wife announced.

"Is that against the law?"

Mrs. Van Klaveren carefully shifted her leg; her ankle was swollen and sore. "Now the poor thing has to drag her brother to the daycare center, while her mother lies around in bed."

"How do you know that?" asked her husband.

"The car's still parked outside, isn't it?" Mrs. Van Klaveren watched as Judith turned the corner. "There's something wrong with that family."

Mr. Van Klaveren knew what was coming, but he'd heard it so many times, he couldn't take it seriously.

"That woman beats her—" Mrs. Van Klaveren began.

"Now, now," Mr. Van Klaveren reassured her. "Don't go making a mountain out of a molehill. Even my father used to give us a good whack every now and again. 'Spare the rod and spoil the child,' he always said."

"Yes, and look how you turned out!"

"They've never given us any trouble, have they? They're gone all day."

"But what about that little girl's screaming and crying?"

"Maybe they've just got the television on too loud," said her husband. "And besides, Trude, a shut mouth catches no flies."

"What's that supposed to mean?"

"It means we should keep our mouths shut and not get involved. How that woman brings up her daughter is her own business, not ours. Look, there's Tilly!"

"Late, as usual," his wife remarked.

"Better late than never."

"What are you, some kind of philosopher?" his wife sneered.

Glad for the distraction, Mr. Van Klaveren shuffled to the front door and opened it before Tilly had even rung the bell.

Judith knocked at the door of the classroom.

"Come in," the teacher called out. Twenty-five pairs of eyes stared at her.

"My ... my mother is sick, so I had ... I had to take my brother to daycare."

"All right, Judith. Go to your seat. We're in the middle of history."

Feeling awkward, Judith made her way to her desk, sat down, and took out her history book. She tried hard to keep her mind on the lesson but couldn't help being aware that Diana was watching her. Diana kept glancing from her to Michael and back again. When the teacher turned around to write something on the blackboard, Diana began whispering to Robert, and then they both looked at Judith and snickered.

At recess, when everyone was pouring out into the school yard, Michael came up to her.

"Hi," he said, trying to act casual. "Get home okay?"

Judith nodded shyly. She wished she could think of something to say, but nothing came to mind. Then Diana dragged her away and started asking her all kinds of questions about Michael: Where did he live? What had they done?

Judith's answers were so vague that Diana finally lost her patience. "What's the point of asking you anything!" she cried in exasperation, and marched off to join the other girls.

Two days later, when Judith was on her way to the school cafeteria, Michael suddenly appeared at her side.

"Wanna come?" he asked.

"Where?"

"Over to my house. You can eat your sandwich there."

Judith stared at him in disbelief. Was he serious?

"So are you coming, or what?" He nodded toward the exit.

"Yes!" cried Judith happily. She still couldn't believe it, but moments later they were racing across the school yard to the bicycle racks.

Just as they did the time before, David and Frank came rushing out the moment the garden gate swung open.

"Judith! Judith!" they shouted, as if she were an old friend. "Did you come to play with us?" They tugged at her jacket.

"Hey, you guys, leave Judith alone. We've gotta eat first."

"And then play, right?" they asked, looking at her hopefully.

"If there's time," Judith promised.

"You don't know what you're saying," Michael warned her. "Now they'll never leave you alone!"

Michael's aunt was in the kitchen making soup; the little girl stood beside her, munching on a rice cracker. Once again, Judith noticed how she gave Michael a kiss and rumpled his hair.

"Hello, Judith. Are you here for lunch?"

She held out one hand and laid the other on Judith's shoulder.

"Hello, ma'am," said Judith softly. "I ... I've already got my own sandwich. Michael asked if I ..." She began stammering.

"How about a bowl of soup to go with it?"
She nodded.
"Okay, why don't the two of you set the table?"
Judith was glad to help out.
"I can tell you've done this before," said Michael's aunt, laughing, when she saw how quickly Judith arranged the plates and glasses.
"Yes, ma'am."
"Children always get worked to death," said Michael. "I mean, look at me. I have to vacuum, make the beds, and do the dishes. There isn't even a dishwasher in this house, can you believe it?"
"You've got it rough," his aunt agreed. "By the way, you forgot to mention the shopping."
"Oh, yeah ... the shopping, all those heavy bags ..." Michael heaved a pitiful sigh.
"And the garden," Aunt Elly added.
"And don't forget the kids. I practically have to raise them myself!" Michael groaned.
He scooped up his cousin, set her down on the counter, and fished a bib out of the drawer.
"Bichael, Bichael ..." she crowed, pulling his hair.
"She's always turning *M*'s into *B*'s," Michael explained to Judith. "A mat is a bat, and a mitten is a bitten. I'm pretty sure she does it on purpose, because she has no trouble at all saying Mommy."
"Mommy," she echoed, pointing to her mother.
"See what I mean?" Michael laughed.
"What's your name?" asked Judith. She was surprised at how easy it was for her to ask that question.
"Bichele!" she cried. "Bichele!"
"That's 'Michele,'" Michael translated.
"She has the same name as Michael, but hers is for a girl," said one of the twins. Judith still couldn't tell them apart. "Right, Mommy?"
His mother nodded.
"I know why her name is Michele," his twin brother began importantly, "because Michael—"

"David, would you hurry up and eat your lunch?" Michael interrupted. "Or we'll be here till suppertime."

But David was determined. "Because Michael—"

"Yeah, yeah, we all know why," Michael cut him off again.

"Not Judith!" David cried indignantly. "Michael brought Michele, didn't he, Mommy?"

"Brought? I think he means 'delivered,'" said his mother, laughing.

"Yeah, out of Mommy's tummy." David (or was it Frank?) pointed proudly at his mother's stomach.

Michael turned red and stubbornly chewed his sandwich. Why did David have to bring that up? You could tell by the look on Judith's face that she didn't know what he was talking about. David's mother noticed, too.

"The baby came so unexpectedly, there was no time to call the doctor. So Michael took over. And here's the result," she said calmly, laying her hand on Michele's head.

"And she had a rope around her neck, too, right, Mommy?" David cried excitedly. After all this time, it was still a thrilling story.

"He means the umbilical cord," his mother explained. "It was wrapped around her neck three times. She didn't cry at first, and a baby's supposed to cry as soon as it's born, you probably know that. Michael immediately saw that something was wrong, and he took charge. A doctor couldn't have done better. Anyway, right after that, she started screaming at the top of her lungs!"

"Wow," was all Judith could say. She was truly impressed. Not just by Michael, but also because they discussed it so openly.

"I want a peanut butter sandwich," shouted David. "And you have to make it." He put a slice of bread on Judith's plate.

"You can do that yourself, David," said his mother.

"Judith can do it herself for me, too."

"Now that's what I call logic," said Michael.

Judith laughed. She fixed David a sandwich, then one for Frank, and wiped off the table when Michele knocked over a glass of milk. She couldn't stop smiling; the hot soup, the laughter, the twins' excited chatter, all made her feel warm and good inside.

When everyone was finished eating, Judith and Michael quickly cleared the table.

"Which would you rather do, wash or dry?" asked Judith as she filled the sink with sudsy water.

"Neither," laughed Michael.

"Okay, you dry." Judith thrust a dishtowel into his hands and began scrubbing away at the dishes.

"That was fast," said Michael when they were done.

"Is that why you invited me over?" teased Judith. What had gotten into her?

"You guessed it," said Michael.

There wasn't enough time left to play with the twins.

"Can you come back tomorrow?" asked Frank.

Judith didn't know what to say; she looked uncertainly at Michael's aunt.

"You can come any time you like, honey," she said. "Right, boys?"

The twins nodded eagerly.

Judith blushed. "See you tomorrow, then," she said.

As they were bicycling back to school, Judith said, "Your aunt is really nice."

"Aunt Elly's cool," Michael agreed. "Uncle Bob, too. And those kids aren't bad either, even though they can drive you crazy sometimes with all that blabbing."

They stopped for a red light.

"You won't tell anybody, will you?" said Michael suddenly.

Judith looked at him. Michael had his eyes fixed on the traffic light.

"About Michele, you mean? That you—"

"Yeah."

"I'm good at keeping secrets."

"I figured you were."

Michael didn't know how true that was.

SEVEN

THAT AFTERNOON, JUDITH RACED HOME IN HIGH SPIRITS. What a great day it had been: first lunch at Michael's, then an A on her essay! "Very good, Judith," Mr. Beekman had said when he handed it back to her.

Her street came into view; just a short sprint, and she was home. Out of breath, she jumped off her bike and wheeled it onto the curb. The curtains in the first-floor window moved as she passed. Without thinking, Judith waved her hand. She was so happy, she felt like waving to everybody.

The expression on Mrs. Van Klaveren's face changed. Slowly, almost hesitantly, she lifted her hand and waved back.

"Who are you waving to?" asked her husband.

"That poor little girl, the one from upstairs. She hasn't got her brother with her. Her mother's probably picking him up. I saw her drive off about fifteen minutes ago."

Judith walked through the narrow alley alongside the house that led to the shed: four wobbly walls and a leaky roof. She carefully locked up her bicycle. Before going inside, she gave one last wave to Mrs. Van Klaveren, who actually smiled. Maybe she wasn't so bad after all, thought Judith. Mommy always complained that she was a grumpy old snoop, but if you had to spend the whole day in a chair by the window, what else could you do?

The house was quiet; her mother must've gone to pick up Dennis.

Judith ran upstairs. Carelessly dumping her schoolbag in the hallway, she opened the living room door and then looked around in amazement. Drawers had been pulled open; papers were lying everywhere, as if someone had been searching the house. There were even papers on the floor. What in the world had happened?

Quickly she gathered up the papers and put them in a pile on the table. Downstairs, a door slammed. Mommy and Dennis? She didn't hear any voices, no little feet pattering up the stairs.

Moments later the living room door flew open. I'm in for it, thought Judith, growing rigid with fear. There was her mother, pale, her lips tight. She headed straight for Judith, who shrank back in terror. She grabbed her arm and dragged her into the hallway.

"Get upstairs." Her voice was deep with pent-up rage. Judith's heart pounded, and her legs turned to jelly. Upstairs meant an even worse punishment; if she screamed, no one could hear her. All the same, Judith obeyed her, and hurried up to her room. There, too, everything had been turned inside out. Clothes, books, notepads, even her piggybank lay in pieces on the floor. The closet in the corner stood wide open. The sheet, she remembered suddenly. Mommy's found the sheet.

She was so dismayed, she didn't even try to dodge the first blow. Her mother smacked her hard across the face. She staggered; two hands grabbed her and began shaking her back and forth.

"You filthy little bitch, give me back my money!"

Judith could hardly think straight. Money? What money?

"Hand it over," her mother spat out. She slapped her again.

"I don't have any money," Judith gasped, holding her hands in front of her face.

"You stole money out of my wallet!" yelled her mother.

"Don't, Mommy, don't ..." begged Judith. "I haven't got any money, I swear ..."

"Still sneaking around behind my back! You didn't think I'd find out, did you?"

"I haven't done anything," sobbed Judith. Oh, if only her mother would stop ...

All of a sudden she did.

"And what do you call this?" she panted. She grabbed the crumpled sheet out of the closet and shoved it triumphantly under Judith's nose. "Stashed away. Bet you didn't think I'd find out about this either. Tried to hide it from me, didn't you? Just like the hundred guilders you pinched from my wallet. Tell me where it is or I'll break your legs!"

"I haven't got it, Mommy. Really! No, not my face, Mommy, not ..."

Judith warded off the blows as best she could, dropping face down on the bed. Her mother's fists hammered into her back and sides.

"Don't, Mommy ... don't," she sobbed.

"Tell me!"

"I don't have it!" screamed Judith.

Suddenly it was over: her mother ran out of the room.

Trembling, Judith got up and locked her door. Then she waited, terrified.

Footsteps ran up the stairs; she heard her mother panting. "Open this door ..." It sounded threatening.

"Mommy, I haven't stolen *anything*. You've got to be-lieve me," Judith pleaded.

"Open it!" Her mother threw herself against the old wooden door, again and again.

The fourth time, the lock gave, and her mother tumbled into the room. In her hand was the metal pipe from the vacuum cleaner.

"Please ... Mommy, please ..." Judith whispered tonelessly. But the first blows were already raining down on her back, her arms, her bottom. She thought it would never end. She stumbled to her bed and buried her head under the pillow, her body huddled in fear.

At last it was over.

She lay there, motionless; she'd even stopped crying. Everything hurt, the blood roared in her ears, her back and bottom were on fire. She wished she didn't exist, that she'd never, ever been born.

There was a dull silence in the rest of the house. Judith tried to sit up. She groaned; her whole body ached. She stared into space, dazed, no longer aware of the mess around her. The front door slammed, jolting her out of her stupor. She heard Dennis's high-pitched voice. Mommy must've picked him up from the daycare center. Judith could tell, by listening, what was going on downstairs:

jacket off—Dennis always wanted to hang it up himself—then his tiny footsteps as he skipped into the kitchen, where he was given something to drink.

Sometime later, there were slow, heavy footsteps on the attic stairs. Judith stiffened, and waited.

The door, which had been open a crack, now opened all the way. She didn't dare look up. But after a while, when nothing happened, she lifted her head.

There was her mother, pale, bleary-eyed. She went over to Judith and sat down next to her on the bed.

At first she said nothing. Judith stared at the floor. She saw her mother's shoes; the toes were turned inward, just like Judith's. Suddenly she heard a quiet sobbing. Her mother was crying. Crying because of her, because she thought she'd stolen her money.

"I ... I didn't do it, Mommy. Really. I didn't steal any money," Judith swore desperately. "And the sheet ... I couldn't help it ..." She began stuttering. "I don't know how it happened. I was sleeping, and when I woke up everything was wet. I wanted to bring it to the laundromat ... and pay with my own money ... and ... and ..."

Her mother's crying upset her so much, she could hardly speak.

"Oh Judith, what are we going to do?" her mother gasped between sobs.

Judith didn't understand; what did she mean?

"I didn't steal any money, Mommy," she began again.

"That's not it, that's not it ..." Her mother swayed back and forth, still sobbing. "I don't want to hurt you," she choked out. "I don't mean to hit you, but it's stronger than I am. I can't stop myself."

Judith was speechless.

"Did I hurt you badly?" It sounded almost humble, and she wiped her eyes.

Judith said nothing.

Hesitantly, her mother put an arm around her shoulder.

"I don't want to hurt you," she repeated, and began sobbing again.

"Please don't cry, Mommy," said Judith, her voice quivering.

"You don't understand, you don't understand." Her mother hid her face in her hands. "How could you, when I don't even understand it myself?"

Despite her exhaustion, Judith couldn't fall asleep. Every time she moved, something hurt. She thought about the last few hours. They'd actually been very pleasant; her mother had done everything she could to cheer Judith up. She'd even bought a whipped cream cake, but the strange thing was, it made Judith sick. The whipped cream was too rich and sweet; she could feel her stomach rising in protest. But since she didn't want to spoil the mood, she forced herself to eat the whole, huge piece her mother had given her. She reached the bathroom just in time, where she threw it all up again. Fortunately, Mommy didn't get mad.

"You're staying home for a couple of days," she decided. "I'll call school tomorrow and tell them you've got a bad stomachache."

She seemed almost relieved with this excuse. Now, at least, there would be a different reason for Judith's absence. In a few days, the welts on her back and arms would be gone, and so would the bruise under her eye.

Mommy hadn't been angry anymore about the sheet, either. "I'll just throw it in the washing machine. That's what it's there for, right?" she said. "Don't worry. It could happen to anybody."

Later that evening, when they were watching television, Nico had called. Judith's mother was on the phone for a very long time.

"Did you know they stole a hundred guilders right out of my wallet?" she told him. "Probably in that bar, remember? When I hung my bag on the back of the chair. What? No, don't be silly, you don't have to do that. I'll be okay. But it's sweet of you to offer."

Then Judith heard her say, "Not tomorrow, Nico. My daughter isn't feeling very well. She's got a bad tummyache. Maybe the day after tomorrow."

When she got off the phone, she was suddenly radiant. "You know what Nico wanted to do? He wanted to give me a hundred guilders because he feels so sorry for me, losing all that money. He thinks it was pickpockets. Can you imagine the nerve of some people? You just can't be too careful."

The rest of the evening her mother had been in high spirits. Judith wished she could be as cheerful, but her stomach was still upset. When she went up to bed her mother made her a hot water bottle, because she was freezing cold.

Judith stared into the darkness. Her eyes stung. Whenever Mommy was nice to her, she always felt like crying. She listened to the sounds from outside: a cat slinking along the roof, a motorcycle tearing noisily down the street.

Now that she wasn't going to school the next day, she wouldn't be able to go to Michael's, either. What a shame; it was always so much fun there. Maybe he'd take somebody else ... Judith sighed. No, she mustn't think about that. She lay very still, and finally fell asleep, but every time she turned over she felt shooting pains in her back. Toward morning, she woke with a start and knew right away what had happened: she'd wet her bed.

EIGHT

MICHAEL COULDN'T HELP FEELING DISAPPOINTED WHEN HE saw that Judith's seat was empty. Was she just late, or was she sick again? She was absent an awful lot. He tried to keep his mind on the geography lesson. Mr. Beekman was telling them about the rain forests, how important they were. Geography was one of Michael's favorite subjects, but all the same, his mind kept wandering.

He really didn't know very much about Judith. She might look like Steffie, the Steffie he remembered, but for the rest, she was completely different. Steffie had been cheerful and open, while Judith was shy and withdrawn. The way I used to be a few years ago, he suddenly realized. That was a strange thought. Judith didn't even have a father, just a mother and a little brother.

He didn't know where she lived, either, but that would be easy enough to find out. He could ask his teacher, or look it up in the phone book. But what if she didn't have a telephone? No, the best thing was to ask Mr. Beekman. Maybe he could even go visit her this afternoon after school! The idea cheered him up.

"You still with us, Michael?" his teacher asked.

"Yes, Mr. Beekman," he answered quickly.

How did his teacher always know when you were thinking about something else? Michael could never understand it.

He focused all his attention on the film they were watching, which showed bulldozers, like ferocious monsters, plowing down a rain forest. Chain saws shrieked, and long tree trunks were carried off in trucks. The inhabitants of the rain forest, who had lived there for centuries, were given a chance to speak. They were angry, desperate people, and Michael deeply sympathized with them. There was also an Englishman, who had lived among them for many years and spoke their language. He was trying to put a stop to the destruction by sabotaging the operations. There was a high price on his head, yet in all those years, no one had ever reported him to the authorities. He hid in the rain forest, moving from place to place, helped by the native people.

When the film was over, the whole class heaved a sigh, including Michael. He was sorry when the bell rang.

Everyone rushed outside, but Michael stayed behind.

"Hey, aren't you coming?" called Robert. "We've got just enough time for a game of soccer."

"You go, I'll be right there."

When he was alone, Michael went up to his teacher. Suddenly shy, he cleared his throat. "Uh ... uh ... I wanted to ask you something."

"Go ahead."

"Do you know Judith's address?"

"Not by heart, but I'll look it up for you if you like." He opened a drawer under his desk and took out a book with the addresses of all his pupils. "Her mother phoned me this morning to say that Judith was sick again. Were you planning to stop by and see her?"

"Maybe," Michael muttered, shrugging his shoulders.

"Here's her address. I'll write it down for you, along with her phone number. Tell her I said hello, and you can let me know how she is tomorrow."

"Okay, Mr. Beekman." Michael turned to leave.

"Oh, wait a minute, Michael ... here." The teacher rummaged around in his drawer again and pulled out a small bag of licorice. "Give this to her, as a get-well present."

Michael hesitated. "But I'm not sure if I'm going or not."

"Just in case."

Michael took the bag of licorice, stuffed it in his pocket, and ran out into the hall.

"Where've you been?" Robert was waiting by the exit, impatiently bouncing a soccer ball.

Michael grinned but didn't answer him.

"With Judith, right?"

"Right."

"Aw, come off it. She wasn't even at school. What's so great about her anyway?"

"Wouldn't you like to know!" Laughing, he snatched the

soccer ball out of Robert's hands and started heading it like a real pro. He could keep that up for hours.

Robert shrugged. That Michael ... Sometimes you just couldn't figure him out.

Judith jumped at the sound of the doorbell.

"Don't let anyone in," her mother had said. "If the bell rings, let it. Don't open the door. And I don't want you going outside either. I'll get Dennis this afternoon."

One look in the mirror told her why she wasn't allowed to go out: the bruise under her eye had turned all the colors of the rainbow.

Her mother was still worried. She'd even phoned from the office to ask how Judith was feeling.

"I'm fine, Mommy," Judith had assured her, "and I hung up the laundry in the stairwell." That way her mother would know that she hadn't even been on the balcony, where she usually hung the wash out to dry. Neither of them said a word about the beating.

One good thing about having to stay home that day: it meant she could wash her dirty sheet, and Mommy would never know she'd wet her bed again. She had opened her bedroom window and stood her mattress up against it, so it would have a chance to dry.

Once again, the shrill sound of the bell; this time it went on ringing, and made her nervous. Who could that be?

Suddenly it stopped; there was a hollow silence. Judith went to the window and peeked through the Venetian blinds. She couldn't see who was standing at the door; she'd have to open the window to do that. The narrow gaps between the slats offered a partial view of the street, which was lined with parked cars. Standing among the cars was a boy in a blue-green jacket. He was just getting on his bike. As she watched, he turned around and looked up. Michael!

Startled, she stepped back from the window. It had been Michael at the door! He'd probably come by to see her.

She flopped down on the sofa. Ow, that hurt. Judith bit her lip.

On the one hand, she was glad she hadn't let him in. Michael would be sure to ask how she'd gotten that bruise, and then she'd have to lie to him. But on the other hand, she thought it was too bad. He'd come especially for her. Nobody else from her new school had ever done that before.

The phone rang; Judith jumped. Could that be her mother again?

"Hello?" she said nervously.

"Hey, where were you?" said an impatient voice on the other end of the line.

For a moment Judith was speechless; it was Michael on the phone.

"I ... I ..." she began.

"Didn't you hear the bell?"

"I ... I ..." Judith stammered again, "where are you?"

"At the butcher's, around the corner. He said I could use his phone. I'll be over in two minutes."

He hung up before she could object.

Judith was desperate. What should she do? The most important thing was to act normal, very normal. And that bruise on her cheek—she'd gotten into a fight yesterday with this kid in the street, and he'd punched her.

She didn't have very long to think about it. The bell rang three times in a row.

"Jesus!" cried Michael. "What happened to you? To your cheek, I mean?"

"Oh, that ..." said Judith, as casually as she could. "I was in a fight ..."

She walked ahead of Michael, up the stairs.

"A fight? With who?"

"Oh, some kids from around here. They wouldn't let me pass."

"How many were there?"

"Three, I think ... or maybe four."

"Jesus," Michael repeated, "what a bunch of creeps. Your cheek's all black and blue." His voice cracked. He wriggled out of his jacket and flung it over the banister. "Does it hurt?" he asked worriedly.

"It's not so bad," said Judith. They walked into the living room.

"Are you home alone?" asked Michael.

"Yes."

"Pretty boring, huh?"

"A little." Suddenly she was very glad that Michael was here. She only hoped he wouldn't ask any more about the bruise. "How did you know where I lived?"

"I got your address from Mr. Beekman. Oh yeah ... I brought something for you." Michael's hand disappeared into his pocket and took out the bag of licorice. "Mr. Beekman asked me to give this to you."

"Wow, that's so nice of him!" cried Judith, blushing.

"And these are from David and Frank." He pulled two crumpled drawings out of the other pocket.

"Wow," Judith said again. She looked at the drawings the twins had done. David had drawn a red train, and Frank, a blue one. In each train sat seven people.

"That's supposed to be us." Michael laughed and pointed to the little figures. "That's Uncle Bob, and Aunt Elly holding Michele. There's you and me. The twins gave themselves the best seats."

Judith felt giddy with happiness. David and Frank had drawn her too, as if she belonged.

"Oh yeah, I've got a present for you from Aunt Elly, too." Michael walked into the hallway and came back with two apples.

"Wow," said Judith, for the third time.

"Can't you think of anything else to say?" asked Michael.

"No," Judith said, laughing.

Michael looked at her. How could such simple gifts make anyone so happy? She was radiant; he'd never seen her this way.

"Do you want something to drink?" she asked.

"Okay," said Michael, flopping down on the sofa. Judith hurried into the kitchen and pulled open the refrigerator door.

"Would you like orange soda, or should I make some tea?" she called out.

Michael came into the kitchen. "Orange soda."
"There's cake, too."
"Great," said Michael.
Judith took out the leftover cake from the night before.
"Mmmm ... whipped cream! At Aunt Elly's, everything's always gotta be healthy, know what I mean? When she bakes an apple pie, you can practically smell the vitamins. The apples have to be organic, too. Whenever we ask her for candy, she gives us dried fruit. Uncle Bob and I get pretty sick of it sometimes, and last summer Uncle Bob said ..." Michael began to laugh. "Last summer, when Aunt Elly asked Uncle Bob to water the garden, he said, 'I thought you liked everything dried!'"
Judith laughed too. "I think your aunt is really nice," she said.
"Yeah, she's okay, as far as the rest goes," Michael admitted. "And luckily, Uncle Bob takes us all out to McDonald's every once in a while, so we can have French fries and hamburgers. And you should see Aunt Elly—she eats more than any of us! 'Heavy on the mayo, right, kids?' she always says."
Judith laughed again and cut a piece of cake for Michael.
"Aren't you having any?"
"No, I better not, I felt pretty nauseous last night."
"Probably because of those creeps. What did your mother say?" asked Michael as they walked back into the living room.
"She was furious," said Judith. It was true, too!
"I can imagine. So what actually happened?"
Judith wished he would stop asking her questions. "Oh, they were just fooling around," she answered vaguely, "and then one of them started hitting me."
"Right in the face. What a jerk. Did they hit you anywhere else?"
Judith shook her head.
"Did anyone try to stop them?"
She shook her head again.
"I can't believe it," Michael cried indignantly. "There you are getting bashed around by a bunch of creeps, and nobody even tries to help you!"

"It all happened so fast," said Judith. She wished Michael would start talking about something else. "How was school?" she asked.

"Okay." Michael shrugged. "Oh yeah, geography was really interesting. But kind of sad, too ... We learned about the rain forests, about how they're chopping them all down." Michael began telling her the whole story; he even forgot to eat his cake. Judith listened quietly and attentively. Suddenly Michael stopped in the middle of a sentence and blurted out, "With that expression on your face, you look just like Steffie!"

"Steffie? Who's that?"

"She was the girl who lived next door to me before we moved to Washington."

"Oh." For a moment Judith wasn't sure how to react.

"We used to play together. She was my best friend. She even gave me a bear."

"What kind of bear?" asked Judith.

"A koala bear. They've only got them in Australia."

"I know," said Judith. "Those are the bears that have some kind of disease. People are afraid they might become extinct."

"Really?"

"Yes. I saw it on TV, there was a program about it. Did she give you the bear for your birthday?"

"No, she just gave it to me ... It was hers, her favorite bear." Michael didn't know why he was telling her this. "I was pretty young—about six, I think." (He'd really been eight.)

"Why did she give her bear away?" asked Judith.

Michael shrugged. "She just did."

"You don't just give away your favorite bear," said Judith.

Michael avoided her eyes and polished off the rest of his cake. When he was finished, he carefully scraped his plate clean.

"Wanna do some homework?" he asked.

"Okay with me," said Judith. She sensed that Michael didn't want to talk about it. "I'll go upstairs and get my books."

When she returned, Michael was looking at a photograph of Dennis, which was standing on top of the television set.

"This is your brother, right?"

"Yes."

"You two don't look at all alike."

"Dennis has a different father," said Judith. "I used to call him Uncle Ben."

"Used to?"

"Yes, he went away. He's got somebody else now." She sounded resigned. "Uncle Ben was a really nice man, though," she added.

"What about your own father?"

"Never met him. He lives somewhere in Germany, I think. My parents got divorced when I was a year old."

"It's not so bad not having a father. You're better off with a mother—that is, if you've got one."

"What do you mean?"

"I've got a father, but if it was up to me, I'd never see him again!" Michael blurted out.

Judith stared at him. How could he say a thing like that? "But why?"

"He was always criticizing me. I never did anything right."

"Is that why you live with your aunt and uncle?"

Michael nodded. "Yeah. A few years ago they came to stay with us in America, and Aunt Elly made a big fuss because I was doing so badly at school. She wasn't mad at me, though, she was mad at my *father* ..." Michael's voice rose triumphantly. "Nobody ever has the guts to stand up to my father, he always knows better, whatever you do, but that didn't stop Aunt Elly. She really let him have it!"

Michael's hands moved nervously, and he cracked his knuckles.

"They all thought I didn't know what was going on. Grownups always think that about kids. Even Aunt Elly can be pretty dumb, as far as that goes, but I can take it from her, because at least she admits it. But not my father, no way. He never admits he's wrong about anything, he thinks he's always right ..."

His knuckles cracked again.

"And that's what Aunt Elly told him, that he always

thought he was right. She screamed so loud, I could hear her up in my room. My father kept saying I was stubborn and a slow learner, and you know what Aunt Elly said? 'Bullshit!' She said 'bullshit,' to my father!"

Michael banged his fists on the table.

"Well, then they really started fighting! Even Uncle Bob got involved. And after that they had a long talk, but they were talking too softly for me to hear. I wish I could've. I was sure my father had blabbed his way out of it, like he always does, but I was wrong! The next day he called me in and asked if I wanted to go back to Holland with Aunt Elly and Uncle Bob. I couldn't believe it! The minute he asked me, I said yes. Anything to get away from him ..."

Michael fell silent. He still didn't know why he was telling her all this. Was it because she looked so much like Steffie?

"Have you been back to America since then?" Judith asked after a while.

"No. My father invited me to come this summer, but I don't want to go. So he's coming here."

"Are you looking forward to seeing him?"

"Are you kidding?" Michael gave a scornful laugh. "Whenever I see him, I hate him so much I can hardly talk. You know what he said to me once?" Michael imitated his father's voice. "'I have the impression that you've completely forgotten how to speak.' That was really mean of him, because, well, I used to stutter a lot, but it stopped when I came back to Holland ..."

"So what did you say?"

"What did I say?" Michael burst out. "Nothing! I wouldn't dare. I don't know what it is, but whenever he's around, my tongue feels like it's tied up in one big knot."

Judith looked at him carefully. Michael's face was red with anger. Suddenly his expression changed.

"I don't even know why I'm blabbing about all this. It's pretty stupid of me."

"I don't think it's stupid," said Judith. "Really."

"Hey, now you look just like Steffie again," said Michael. "She was great. But ... you are, too."

Judith was so flustered, she didn't know which way to look. "Do you ... do you want some more cake?" she stammered shyly.

Michael laughed. "That's not why I said it. But I wouldn't mind another piece."

Judith jumped up, and winced. For a moment she'd completely forgotten about the pain in her back.

"What's wrong?" asked Michael.

"I ... I just felt really hungry all of a sudden," she lied. "Maybe I will have some of that cake."

NINE

WHAT A STRANGE AFTERNOON, MICHAEL THOUGHT AS HE RODE home on his bike. But he couldn't really say why. Judith's mother had called school and told them Judith was sick, but she'd said nothing about the boys who had beaten her up. Michael tightened his lips. Those creeps, he thought, he'd like to see them try that when he was around. And nobody had done a thing to help her! There had been three or four of them, Judith had told him, but she'd seemed unwilling to say any more about it. Michael had the feeling that all she wanted to do was forget the whole incident. What he didn't understand was why Judith and her mother hadn't gone straight to the police to show them how badly beaten she was.

Michael remembered how Judith had bent down to get some books out of her schoolbag. She was wearing a faded T-shirt with long sleeves, and when she leaned over, it slid up and exposed part of her back. He was shocked at what he saw.

"What happened to your back?" he cried.

Judith had turned bright red and quickly pulled down her T-shirt. "Oh, it's nothing," she mumbled.

"Nothing?" He jumped up and grabbed her arm.

"Ow!" She winced as Michael pushed up her sleeve.

He gasped. "You're all black and blue!" And then he, too, turned red, with rage and indignation.

Judith tried to laugh it off, but he could see that she was very confused. "You won't ... you won't tell anyone, will you?" She blinked nervously.

"Why not?"

"Because ... because, uh, I just don't want them to know."

"You mean the kids at school?"

Judith nodded.

"But I can tell Mr. Beekman, can't I? And Aunt Elly?"

She'd stared at the floor, saying nothing.

"You can tell them, they'll understand. Listen, all that stuff about my father, about how he never listens and all that ... I'd only tell that to you, nobody else has to know. But if I'd been pulverized by a bunch of sleazeballs like that, I'd go around telling everybody!"

Michael grimly pedaled on. They'd better not try anything like that again, he thought, 'cause if they do, they'll be sorry.

"Hey, I've got an idea," he'd said to Judith. "Why don't I ride home with you after school? They won't lay a hand on you if I'm around."

Judith had gazed at him silently with that pitiful black eye. Her fingers toyed nervously with a pencil; she looked just like a little girl.

Maybe that was it, thought Michael. You always had the feeling you had to stand up for her, protect her, even though she never asked you to, probably *because* she never asked you to. With Steffie it had been just the opposite: she had stood up for *him*—to his father, no less. Steffie and Judith ... They might look alike, but for the rest, they were very different.

Michael thought about how they'd done their homework together. Judith had patiently read him the history lesson, several times, so he'd remember it. He tried to listen, but now and then he had trouble, because he was paying too much attention to her: the way she read, with a serious expression on her face, her head bent over the book as she followed the words with her index finger. Whenever she came to a difficult word, a note of doubt crept into her voice and her finger stopped. Slowly, haltingly, she'd read it over again. Her straight blond hair fell across her face; every so often she swept it back. She had circles under her eyes, as if she hadn't slept well. And that bruise ... Every time he looked at it he got a funny feeling in his stomach, and his fists clenched.

Michael was so lost in thought, he almost rode through a red light. He braked just in time but skidded into the bike of the person riding next to him.

"Sorry, ma'am," Michael mumbled.

"Hate to disappoint you, kid, but I'm a man!" said a friendly voice.

"Oh. Sorry about that too," Michael mumbled.

"Bumps into my bike, thinks I'm a she ... Hey, you're in love, right?" The man looked at him; he was young, and everything about his face seemed to be laughing.

"Uh ... uh ..." Michael stuttered.

The light turned green.

"Well, you may not be, but *I* sure am!" The man gave Michael a hearty pat on the back, then shot off on his bike. Michael turned right, chuckling. In love? Him? Come on! Feeling strangely elated all of a sudden, he raced home.

"For me?" Judith could hardly believe it. She stared at the plastic bag her mother had thrust into her hands. It was like a birthday party, everyone showering her with gifts—even her mother!

"Me car," Dennis announced, proudly showing her his new fire engine.

"You've got a present, and so does Judith," said her mother as she peeled him out of his jacket.

Judith's hand disappeared into the plastic bag. "Oooh ..." she breathed, taking out a red sweater.

She held it up to see how it looked. "For me?" she asked again.

Her mother nodded. Judith tried to give her a kiss, but she turned around and walked into the hallway to hang up her coat. Judith stood there awkwardly, still holding the sweater.

"Thank you, Mommy," she said timidly when her mother returned. Should she try to kiss her again? No point; she was already on her way to the kitchen.

"Anything interesting happen today?" her mother called out.

Once again Judith hesitated. Should she tell her that Michael had dropped by? No, she'd better not; that would definitely spoil the mood.

"Nothing special," Judith called back. She'd been careful to erase every trace of Michael's visit: she'd rinsed the glasses, cleared away the books, and hidden the licorice in her schoolbag. There was no sign that anyone had been here.

Only the cake, but if she was lucky, her mother wouldn't notice. Besides, Judith could always say she'd had an extra big piece.

Judith followed her mother into the kitchen.

"It's a beautiful sweater, Mommy," she said.

"And it wasn't cheap, either," said her mother. "I saw it in the window and I thought: I'm going to buy that for my daughter." She didn't look at Judith as she spoke; she was talking to the teakettle.

"So I went inside. The saleslady said, 'I'm afraid you'll have to wait a week for that sweater, ma'am, because that's the last one I've got and I can't take it out of the window. The window dresser is coming in a week to redo the display, and then I can put it aside for you.' But I said to her, 'I don't want to wait a week, I want it now. It's a present for my daughter.' And then she started whining all over again about the window dresser and I said, 'Let me speak to the manager.' So the manager walked in—a real slimeball—and tried to palm me off with a different sweater, but I wasn't giving in: it was either that sweater or no sweater at all. Finally they called in this skinny little guy—he looked like one of those store dummies himself!—and *he* had to get the sweater. He crawled through the window on his hands and knees: you should've seen all the people watching! But at least I got my sweater." Her mother laughed triumphantly at the teakettle.

"Can I try it on?"

"That's what it's for," said her mother.

Judith ran to the mirror in the hallway and pulled off her T-shirt. She tried to ignore the pain in her back, the bruises on her arms and shoulders. Quickly she picked up the sweater and slipped it over her head. It was soft and roomy, and the warm color seemed to light up her face. It made her feel strangely happy.

She walked back into the kitchen. "Look, Mommy," she cried, "how beautiful ..."

Judith's mother turned around and stared at her. There was an odd expression on her face, a mixture of shock and fear, but it quickly passed. Her eyes grew hard. "Take that sweater off this minute," she snarled, "and give Dennis a bath."

Judith was confused, but she did what her mother said. She went back into the hallway, took off the sweater, and carefully folded it. After the sweater, her old T-shirt felt very ordinary. She led Dennis into the bathroom and ran the water for his bath. He chattered away in his unintelligible gibberish, but Judith was only half listening. Why did she have to take off the sweater? Maybe Mommy was worried that she might get it dirty. She'd gone to so much trouble to buy it for her; she'd even had it specially removed from the shop window. "It's a present for my daughter," Mommy had said. Whenever Mommy talked about "her daughter," she always seemed to be talking about somebody else—not about her. And she never looked at her when she said it, either, Judith had noticed. But Mommy often bought her something after she'd beaten her, as if to make up for what she'd done.

Judith dried Dennis off and helped him into his pajamas. Then she set the table.

All through dinner, her mother was silent and distracted. Judith remained on her guard; she knew this mood could take a sudden turn.

Just before going to bed, she said, "Good night, Mommy, and thanks for the beautiful sweater."

Once again Judith tried to give her mother a kiss, but she began groping around for her cigarettes. The lighter clicked. "Okay, okay, that's enough," her mother muttered irritably, fanning away a cloud of smoke.

Nothing's changed, but everything seems different, Judith thought. Was it because she'd been going home with Michael every day for lunch? That hour was the high point of her day. Michele and the twins came rushing up to her the moment she walked through the gate, and Aunt Elly—as she'd also started calling Michael's aunt—treated her as if she belonged. That was the nicest part of all: the ease with which she'd been accepted into Michael's family. At first it had confused her, and she wasn't sure how to respond. The way Aunt Elly put her arm around your shoulder and gave you a kiss, just like that! She still had to get used to it. Michael wasn't surprised; he thought it was perfectly normal.

The funny thing was that, even at school, she felt more like she belonged. Diana may have been jealous of her friendship with Michael, yet even she had begun treating her differently. She still asked a lot of questions about him, but Judith kept her answers vague. She didn't even have that much to tell; there was nothing unusual going on. The two of them just biked over to his house and ate lunch with the rest of the family; afterward, she and Michael cleared the table and washed the dishes. But what she enjoyed most, what she could never explain to Diana, was the way they all got along with each other. Not that there were never any arguments; Frank and David often squabbled, and Judith was surprised one day to hear Michael talking back to his aunt.

"You're being so unfair!" he'd burst out at her.

"I know, and I don't care," she snapped. "I'm in a lousy mood."

"As if we didn't know," Michael said, laughing, and before long his aunt was laughing too. Judith couldn't believe it; she didn't know such things were possible!

After school Michael usually cycled part of the way home with her. One day he asked her to show him the place where the boys had beaten her up. That was very awkward for Judith; she hated lying to Michael, but she had no choice. He always rode with her as far as the daycare center and then raced back to the swimming club for practice. Actually, Judith was glad he didn't take her all the way home; she was scared her mother might find out about their friendship.

At home she said nothing about her visits to Michael's house. For all her mother knew, she still ate lunch at school.

But every now and then Mommy would give her a suspicious look, as if she sensed a change in her. She never said anything, though. This went on for more than a week, until one night, in the middle of supper, she suddenly remarked,

"I get the feeling you're hiding something from me."

Judith was so shocked, she nearly choked on her food. Just then, thank goodness, the phone rang; it was Nico.

Judith had met him twice, but never for long, because Mommy always sent her up to her room. She didn't feel comfortable with him, even though he really tried to be nice. The time before, he'd even brought her a chocolate bar.

Was it his piercing voice that bothered her, or his restless gaze? He'd come over that night, too, to take her mother out. Her mother had gone off in high spirits. Judith was glad to see her looking so happy; it didn't happen often.

Mommy smelled so good, too. Each time she walked through the living room, she left behind a faint flowery scent that lingered in the air long after she was gone.

Judith was awakened by the front door slamming. She heard stumbling on the stairs, whispering, and a stifled laugh from her mother. The light went on in the hallway, and a pale yellow streak fell through the half-open door into her room. Once again, she heard whispers and giggles.

"Not so loud, Dennis is asleep," her mother warned in a low voice. Then they disappeared into the living room.

By this time Judith was wide awake. Her alarm clock said quarter to one. She sat up; she had to go to the bathroom. As quietly as she could, she slid out of bed. Just when she'd reached the stairs, the living room door opened. It was Nico.

Judith stepped back and waited. Was he leaving? She leaned over the banister and saw him standing next to the coatrack. Quick as a flash, his hand dived into her mother's bag, snatched something out, and stuffed it in his pocket. Then he turned around and disappeared into the bathroom.

Judith's heart pounded. What had Nico taken out of Mommy's bag? Money? The toilet flushed, and moments later she heard him going back into the living room. Her heart was still pounding as she tiptoed down the stairs. She cast a quick glance at her mother's old brown bag. The toilet was still gurgling. She didn't flush when she was through, so they wouldn't know she was up.

Judith lay awake for a long time afterward, worrying. What should she do if Mommy found out there was more money missing? She broke out in a cold sweat. If she were to tell her what she'd seen, her mother would never believe her. She'd think she was just trying to get Nico in trouble, and then Judith herself would get the blame. She clenched her fists helplessly. Clammy fear crept up and grabbed her by the throat. She stared into the darkness, and her head began to throb.

At two-thirty she heard Nico leaving. Then she dozed off, but kept jolting awake with a sense of panic. Her mind was filled with confused, feverish dreams. Finally she sank down, deep, deep down, until, far off in the distance, she heard someone calling her name.

"Judith!" The sound came closer.

Still half asleep, she sat up and blinked her eyes. Her mother was standing in the doorway.

"Come on, lazybones," she sang out, "time to get up." She turned back the quilt and stared, horrified, at the sheets. "Again?"

Judith didn't have to ask; she knew what had happened. She'd wet her bed. Again.

TEN

MICHAEL COULDN'T KEEP HIS MIND ON THE HISTORY LESSON. He could hear his teacher's voice, but the words weren't getting through to him. He sat there chewing his pen and wondering what was wrong with Judith.

That morning she'd arrived at school just before the bell rang and had gone quietly to her seat. Usually when she came in she turned and gave him a quick smile, but not today.

Judith was always trying not to attract attention, thought Michael. You really had to know her to understand her. She never said much, and he often had to guess, by a gesture or the expression on her face, what she was thinking or feeling. Sometimes she'd suddenly have the strangest look, as if she were wounded. A wounded look ... what made him think of that?

He peeked at her out of the corner of his eye. She seemed worried about something.

Then Michael's eyes met his teacher's. Don't say anything, Michael begged silently, please just leave her alone. "As I was saying," Mr. Beekman went on calmly, "on December 7th, 1941, a fleet of Japanese carriers attacked the United States navy base at Pearl Harbor. This marked the beginning of American involvement in World War II."

Michael breathed a sigh of relief and tried to concentrate on the rest of the lesson.

While his pupils were busy doing a grammar exercise, Mr. Beekman corrected their math homework. Now and then he glanced around the room. He saw Michael plodding away, and when Michael looked up, sighing, he gave him an encouraging nod. Michael made a face, and his teacher smiled.

Mr. Beekman hadn't failed to notice the growing friendship between Michael and Judith, and he was glad about it. Michael, despite his learning disability, was one of the most popular kids in the class. When he took someone under his wing, the rest of the class accepted it. There had been the usual teasing, of course, but it hadn't lasted long, probably because Michael was so matter-of-fact about the whole thing. Judith, who was always so quiet anyway, just kept silent and pretended not to hear them.

His eyes rested briefly on her. She looked terrible, as if she hadn't slept a wink. In spite of all his good intentions, he still hadn't phoned her mother. But in two weeks it would be Parents' Night. He'd give Judith a note for her mother, urging her to come.

At lunchtime, the two children rode their bikes to Michael's house.

"Is something wrong?" asked Michael. He had to repeat it twice before Judith looked at him, frightened.

"No, no ..." she stammered, leaning farther over the handlebars.

There *was* something wrong, thought Michael, but she wouldn't say what.

"Don't you like coming over for lunch anymore?" Now she looked even more frightened. She began swerving, and they nearly crashed into each other.

"That's not it," said Judith. How could he think such a thing!

"Then there is something wrong," Michael persisted.

Judith nodded silently.

Michael braked and got off his bike.

"Flat tire?" Judith looked back.

"No."

She braked too, and waited.

"Why won't you tell me what it is?" asked Michael. He sounded hurt.

Judith started kicking her bicycle tire, trying to hide her uneasiness.

"It's all so complicated." She sighed.

"What's so complicated?"

"It's ... my mother ..." Judith began hesitantly. "She ... she's got a new boyfriend. She met him a few weeks ago."

Judith had stopped kicking the tire and was now polishing her bicycle bell with the sleeve of her sweater.

"So what's the matter? Don't you like him?"

"Not really," Judith admitted, "but that's not the only thing."

The polishing grew more emphatic. Michael waited.

"A while ago, my mother noticed she was missing a hundred guilders. Nico—that's her boyfriend's name—had taken her out to eat, and the next day when she looked in her wallet, the money was gone. She thought somebody had stolen it, in the restaurant where they'd eaten. Nico thought it was probably pickpockets. That had happened to him once, too. Anyway, last night they went out again, and when they came home ..."

Judith told him what she'd seen. Michael's expression changed from one of concern to one of outrage.

"What a lousy thing to do! Have you told your mom?"

"No, not yet."

She sounded very unhappy; you could tell she was worried about it.

"My mother was so glad she finally had a boyfriend again. And maybe it's not true, maybe he was taking something else out of her bag. Right?" She looked at Michael hopefully.

"You'll find out soon enough," said Michael. "Your mother'll notice if there's any money missing."

Judith's face clouded over. That's just it, she thought. And Michael couldn't imagine how much that frightened her.

"If the money *is* missing, the best thing is to tell her right away what you saw," Michael advised. "But I can understand if that worries you. It's never any fun having to tell somebody something like that."

"No," sighed Judith.

They pedaled on, but it wasn't until she was sitting in Michael's kitchen with the twins, who demanded all her attention, that she was able to put it out of her mind.

That afternoon Judith cycled home by herself. Michael never went with her on Tuesdays because he had to do extra practice.

"Good luck," Michael had whispered in her ear when the bell rang and everybody ran outside. She smiled at him gratefully. He hadn't forgotten.

When she rang the bell at the daycare center, Sophie opened the door.

"Come on in," said Sophie warmly. "I've just made tea. Would you like some?"

Sophie walked into the kitchen, followed by a couple of giggling children. "Dennis was kind of droopy today," she told Judith when she returned with the tea. "I'll bet he's coming down with the flu. He wasn't very hungry, either."

Just then Dennis appeared in the doorway, sucking his thumb. He walked up to Judith and climbed into her lap.

"I think he's got a fever," said Judith. "He feels so warm."

Sophie watched as Judith lay her hand on his forehead and stroked his hair. There was something almost motherly about her concern for him. Even the way she let him drink from her cup.

"Where's Michael? Couldn't he make it today?" Sophie asked.

"He's got extra practice on Tuesday," Judith told her. "He belongs to a swimming club, and he does basketball, too. His whole room is full of posters, especially swimming posters."

"Seems like a nice guy," said Sophie. "I've only met him once, but I was impressed."

"He is nice," Judith agreed. "His aunt, too. It's so much fun at his house." As she began enthusiastically telling her about it, her whole face changed; she seemed to grow younger. She's just a very little girl, thought Sophie all of a sudden. Judith's eyes shone as she talked about Frank and David and the drawings they'd made for her. As if it were something really special. She chattered on and on, and Sophie listened, smiling.

"Sounds to me like you feel right at home there," said Sophie when Judith paused to catch her breath. "But why does Michael live with his aunt and uncle?"

"He doesn't have a mother."

"Oh. That's sad. What about his father?"

"He lives in America."

"Doesn't he miss him?" asked Sophie.

"No. They don't get along very well." The words were out before she knew it.

"That's sad, too." Sophie sighed. "Good thing he's got his aunt and uncle. And what about you? Do you get along with your dad?"

The question came as such a surprise that Judith hardly had time to think.

"I ... I don't know him. My parents are divorced. I think he lives in Germany."

"Well, he doesn't know what he's missing," said Sophie. "But at least you've still got your mother."

"Yes." Judith leaned over Dennis, so that Sophie couldn't see the expression on her face. Dennis slid down off Judith's lap and tugged at her sleeve.

"He's had enough for today," said Sophie. "He wants to go home. If I were you, I'd put him right to bed."

Sophie helped him into his jacket and wrapped his scarf three times around his neck.

"Please don't tell Mommy about Michael, okay?" asked Judith as Sophie walked them to the door.

"You mean she doesn't know about him yet?" Sophie asked, surprised.

"No ... uh ... if I told her, she'd start teasing me. About him being my boyfriend. The kids at school do that too, sometimes."

"Aw, that's not so bad," said Sophie encouragingly.

"No ... uh ... but you won't tell her, will you?" she begged.

"I won't say a word."

Judith's face cleared.

Something's wrong, thought Sophie as she watched them go. But she couldn't say what it was.

The silence in the house made Judith nervous. She kept looking up at the clock. Ten past five: forty-five minutes to go before her mother got home. Dennis was slumped in an armchair; he didn't feel like going to bed. Judith had tucked a blanket around him. She paced restlessly up and down the room. Should she get started on her homework?

She tried doing some math problems, but she was so tense, she couldn't concentrate. Maybe she was worrying about nothing, she tried to tell herself. Maybe it was all a big misunderstanding. But if that were true, why was she so cold, and why were her palms so clammy?

Five-thirty ... What if she did some vacuuming? It had to be done anyway, and it would drive away the ominous silence.

Judith went to the hall closet and took out the vacuum cleaner. Moments later the dull roar filled the living room. Her arms moved automatically, back and forth; her eyes were fixed on the ground. The steady drone filled her head, too, and gradually calmed her down. Nothing's going to happen, she kept telling herself, nothing at all.

She didn't hear the footsteps on the stairs, or the door opening.

Suddenly a hand grabbed her roughly by the hair and yanked back her head. Judith screamed in terror and pain; she was completely unprepared for this, and even forgot to protect her face. Her mother dragged her into the kitchen and began punching, stomping, kicking. Judith couldn't move; she was pinned to the counter, her arms crossed in front of her face.

"You disgusting thief," her mother hissed. "You sneaky little bitch." Each word was followed by a blow.

"Mommy, Mommy, don't ..."

"You've stolen my money again!" her mother shrieked. "*You're* the one who's been robbing me. You, you, you!"

"I didn't do it! It was Nico!" Judith screamed desperately.

For a moment her mother stared at her, speechless. Then her face darkened; it grew ugly with rage. She reached out, opened a drawer, and grabbed the rolling pin. Judith was just able to turn around. She felt the wood beating down on her back and shoulders, then a powerful blow to her head ...

ELEVEN

MICHAEL WAS ON HIS WAY TO THE SWIMMING POOL. HE PEDALED as fast as he could. Swimming was his favorite sport; after that came basketball, and then running. He was good at all three, but he liked swimming best; in the water, he felt strong and free. When they'd first come to live in the Hague, he'd joined a swimming club, and it wasn't long before Mr. Rovers, the coach, let him swim in league matches, where he did surprisingly well.

"You can do even better," said Mr. Rovers, "but you'll have to work at it!"

Michael arrived at the pool: a modern, sand-colored building. He put his bike in the rack, locked it up, and ran inside. Already, he could hear voices echoing in the tiled hall, a loud splash as somebody dived into the pool, the shrill sound of Mr. Rover's whistle.

He ducked into the locker room and came out a few minutes later in his swimming trunks. Mr. Rovers was swaggering back and forth along the edge of the pool, shouting instructions to a boy in the water. When he caught sight of Michael, he held up his hand, then turned back to the pool. Michael dived in, and soon he was gliding smoothly through the water. He'd try to make a good time today. He always did his best to impress Mr. Rovers, who glowed with pride whenever you improved your personal record. Not that it made much sense, Michael sometimes thought. Who cared about a tenth of a second? But still ...

Michael heard the familiar whistle. He looked up and saw Mr. Rovers signaling to him.

"Could you get out here for a minute?" he shouted. "I wanna talk to you!"

Michael climbed out of the pool and shook his wet hair. He went over to the bench where Mr. Rovers was sitting.

"Do you know Peter Stijn?"

What a question! Everybody knew him. He was the junior division club champion.

"Sure I do!"

"Well, that sonofabitch is going to New Zealand. For good. What would anybody wanna go there for?" Mr. Rovers looked at Michael accusingly.

"The kid just goes off and leaves me ..." He leaned forward, his elbows on his knees, and began fiddling with his stopwatch. "Leaves me here with you," he finished, turning to Michael. For the first time Michael noticed what a big, wide nose he had; it took up a large portion of his face.

"You know what that means, don't you? You'll have to take his place," Mr. Rovers went on impatiently, as if Michael should've understood that by now.

"*Me?*" Michael gasped. "But Peter Stijn's the champ!"

"So what?" snapped Mr. Rovers.

"I'm a year younger than he is." His voice cracked.

"All the better. You'll have to train three times as hard. No more fooling around. From now on, you've gotta work your butt off. I want you here every day for practice. Morning and evening."

"What about Martin? Why don't you ask him? He made a better time than I did last week." Michael pointed toward Martin, who was just disappearing into the locker room.

"That's because you weren't concentrating hard enough." Mr. Rovers was right, Michael suddenly thought. He hadn't been concentrating. "Besides, you're tougher than Martin, you've got more stamina."

Michael was speechless. He wasn't used to hearing praise from Mr. Rovers.

"Well?" Mr. Rovers frowned at him. "What're we waiting for?"

"Do you ... do you really think I can do it?"

Mr. Rovers brought his big nose threateningly close to Michael's face.

"Think? *Think?* If I only *thought* you could do it, I wouldn't have asked you. I know!"

He grabbed Michael's arm and led him to the edge of the pool.

"In you go," he ordered. "We've wasted enough time already."

Half an hour later, Michael climbed out of the pool, panting. He'd obediently followed all his coach's instructions, and he was exhausted.

But it still wasn't good enough for Mr. Rovers. "That was pathetic!" he boomed. "I hope you're in better shape tomorrow morning. I want you here at quarter to seven, sharp. We're gonna do some leg exercises." His wide nose gleamed with satisfaction.

They walked toward the locker room. Suddenly Michael stopped; the blood rushed to his head. There, on a bench against the tiled wall, sat his father! He got up and came over to them.

"Hello, Michael."

Michael inadvertently took a step backward. "Hi, Dad," he mumbled. He darted a glance at the locker room. "Be right back. Gotta get changed," he said quickly, and ran off.

Mr. Rovers was puzzled. What had gotten into that boy? He turned to the man standing next to him. "You Michael's father?"

"Yes."

"Good kid, that son of yours. Natural-born swimmer. With the right training, he'll go far. Very far."

They sat down on the bench. Mr. Rovers talked, and Michael's father listened, his eyes fixed on the locker room door. It was a long time before Michael came out again. His wet hair was tousled, his shoulders bowed. He stood by the door, waiting.

The two men got up and went over to him. Mr. Rovers put his hand on Michael's shoulder and gave him an encouraging squeeze. "We'll try again tomorrow, okay, Michael?"

"Okay, Mr. Rovers," he answered meekly. He stared down at the floor and then followed his father to the exit.

Mr. Rovers thoughtfully rubbed his nose. All of a sudden that kid was acting like a whipped dog. A whipped dog! What the hell was wrong?

Michael and his father walked down the street, in silence. When they reached the corner, Michael suddenly remembered that he'd left his bicycle at the pool.

"I forgot my bike," he stammered, and ran back. As if things weren't bad enough, he thought. Now his father would see what a jerk he still was. He rummaged nervously through his pockets for his key and stuck it in the padlock.

When he got back, his father didn't say a word. He's probably saving it all up, Michael thought bitterly, so he can wipe the floor with me when we get home. He peeked at him out of the corner of his eye. His father was going gray, he noticed, and he was dressed differently, too. More casual. Instead of a shirt and tie, he was wearing a sweater, as if he were on vacation.

"Can I buy you something to drink?" his father offered.

"Okay." Michael didn't sound very enthusiastic.

A short while later they were sitting opposite each other in a coffee shop. His father ordered tea, and he had a Coke.

"Do Aunt Elly and Uncle Ben know you're in Holland?" asked Michael.

"Yes. Elly told me you were at practice, and she gave me the address of the pool. I didn't know you were such a good swimmer."

Michael shrugged. There's a lot you don't know, he thought, staring out the window. The trees already had buds on them. "But sports aren't important." Michael thought he'd found just the right tone: flippant, as if he couldn't care less.

"Who told you that?"

"*You* did!" Michael burst out angrily. Oh, this was great. Now he was pretending he'd never even said it!

His father took a slow sip of his tea, then put down his cup. "Yes," he said, shaking his head, "that was stupid of me."

Had he heard right? Michael eyed his father suspiciously.

"Pretty shortsighted, too, don't you think?"

Was he being serious, or was this some kind of a trap?

"I may not be much of a sportsman myself, but that doesn't mean that sports aren't important." He paused. "There must've been times when you really hated me, Michael. And I can't say I blame you."

Michael was silent; he couldn't believe his ears. Maybe this was a trick—maybe he had to go back to America!

"That coach believes in you. He says you have talent. You'd never know it, though, the way he was telling you off back there in the pool."

Michael's face changed; the tension and suspicion disappeared. "He always does that," he said. "Boy, can he swear! You should hear him cursing at Peter Stijn. Peter's the club champion, but Mr. Rovers calls him every name you can think of. But he doesn't mean it. The more he screams, the more he likes you."

His father smiled. "Do you still play basketball?"

"Yeah, but I'll have to cut down a little, because Mr. Rovers wants me to come train every day. But we do basketball at school. And running, too."

"Jogging?"

"Yeah, but I like real running better. On Field Day we're having a race. Three boys from my class were chosen to take part."

"Are you one of them?"

Michael nodded. He didn't know what make of all this. There was his father, sitting right across from him and asking him about sports ... He'd never shown the slightest interest before.

"I've started jogging, too," his father told him.

"*You?*" Michael's mouth dropped open.

"Yes, me." His father looked almost bashful and began fiddling with his spoon. "I thought it was about time I got in shape."

Michael was completely bewildered. This was getting crazier by the minute.

"That must come as a surprise," said his father.

"You can say that again! Actually, you do look kind of different. More ... more ..." He hesitated.

"More what?"

"More relaxed."

"That's the way I feel, too," admitted his father.

"Is that because of the jogging?"

"Yes, that may be part of it. But I think it has more to do with Helen."

There was a silence. All of a sudden Michael felt queasy, and he stared down at his empty glass.

So that was it. His father had a girlfriend. Somehow he'd always thought of his father as being alone. First there was his mother—but those memories were too vague. After that there was only his father, big and powerful. A father he could never stand up to, who always made him feel small and stupid. That old, treacherous feeling took hold of him again, seized him by the throat. What did his father want? To take him back to America? Never!

His father gazed at him for a while. He saw the wary look on Michael's face.

"You met her once, many years ago, In Washington."

Michael remained silent. He couldn't think. Didn't want to, either. He couldn't care less who she was.

"Do you remember the time you ran away? You were gone a whole night. I was certain you'd had an accident ..."

His father's voice faltered.

"The next morning I got a telephone call from a woman. You'd spent the night in her garage, in her car. Well ... that woman is Helen."

Michael's heart pounded. He stared hard at his glass. He could remember everything about that day and night, how scared and lonely he'd been. How frightened he was the next morning when that woman had found him and taken him into her kitchen, where she'd made him breakfast.

"Why did you run away?" she'd asked.

"Because I'm stupid," he'd answered.

But she hadn't thought he was stupid, not at all. She'd thought he was smart, because he'd found an unlocked garage and slept in the car. She'd been very friendly, and her kitchen was small and sunny. And now this woman, whose name turned out to be Helen, was his father's girlfriend.

"Yeah, I remember her," he mumbled, trying to sound indifferent.

"She remembers you, too," his father went on. "We ran

into each other in a drugstore, after I'd been transferred back to Washington. She was standing behind me in line, and she tapped me on the shoulder. 'Aren't you Michael's father?' she asked. That surprised me—she didn't say Mike, like everyone else there used to call you. She said Michael. With an American accent. It sounded kind of nice. Anyway, I had no idea who she was. The morning I picked you up, I was so relieved to have found you, I hardly paid any attention to her. I thanked her, of course, and apparently I even sent her flowers—she told me that later on—but I'd forgotten about that too. 'Has he been running away lately?' she asked, and that's when it began to dawn on me. She asked me how you were, and I told her you were living in Holland. Before we knew it we were having a cup of coffee and talking about everything under the sun. I haven't felt that comfortable with anyone in years."

There was a long silence.

"Does she still live in the same house?" Michael finally asked.

"Yes."

"And does she still have an apple tree in the garden?"

"That, too."

"And is she still a gym teacher?"

His father laughed. "Yes, and she still remembers you telling her that I thought gym wasn't important. She thought that was an unbelievably stupid thing to say, and she also said you could tell what I thought just by looking at me, because I was way out of shape, and that it was about time I started jogging. So that's what I did."

His father gave a funny, helpless shrug.

"Would you like another Coke, Michael? Or something else?" he asked.

"No, thanks." Michael hesitated. "I don't have to go back to America now that you've got a girlfriend, do I?" he asked suspiciously.

"No, of course not." Now it was his father who hesitated. "But you can come visit whenever you like. I hope ... I hope that maybe you'll spend a vacation with us sometime, so we can have the chance to ... to get to know each other again."

Michael nodded firmly. He was relieved that his father didn't try to talk him into anything. "How long are you staying in Holland?"

"One night, that's all. I'm just passing through on my way to Frankfurt."

"Are you staying at our house?"

"No, I've already booked a hotel."

"Are you coming over for dinner?"

"Yes."

"Then don't get your hopes up," said Michael drily, "'cause you and me are gonna have to do the cooking."

"I do almost all the cooking nowadays," said his father.

"*You?*"

"Yes, me. Didn't know I had it in me, did you?"

"No," said Michael, laughing.

His father called the waiter over to ask for the check, and a few minutes later they were standing outside.

What a weird evening, thought Michael as he lay in bed. It was late, but he couldn't fall asleep; there was too much on his mind.

He couldn't figure out what had happened to his father; it was as if he'd suddenly become a normal person. Even Aunt Elly and Uncle Bob had kept staring at him in amazement.

"What's wrong with you, Dirk?" Aunt Elly had asked him at the table.

"What do you mean?"

"You haven't made an insulting remark all evening."

His father chuckled. "I was just about to compliment you on your culinary skills."

"Ah, that's better! For a moment there, I was scared that you'd forgotten how to be nasty."

Smiling, Aunt Elly took another bite of the spaghetti his father had cooked. "If you ask me, there's a woman involved. What do you think, Bob?"

"I can't think, I'm busy," mumbled Uncle Bob. He fished a few strands of spaghetti out of David's hair. "When is this son of ours going to learn how to eat properly?"

"Give him time," said Aunt Elly unconcernedly. "So, Dirk, is there a woman involved?" She looked at Michael's father, who smiled mysteriously but said nothing.

"That's a definite yes," Aunt Elly decided. "I like her already. You're looking a whole lot better, you know."

"Was it that bad?" asked his father.

"Yes. But I just couldn't make you see that."

"You certainly tried."

Aunt Elly grinned. "I still don't understand how she could fall for you."

"She fell for my cooking. I served her one of your world-famous recipes."

They went on like that for a while, until Uncle Bob finally cried, "Would you two cut that out?"

Michael just sat there listening. Aunt Elly often teased his father, but he usually couldn't take it. He'd lash out at her with some sarcastic remark, and they'd end up arguing. But that hadn't happened this evening; everyone was very relaxed.

Later, when Michele and the twins were in bed and Michael was allowed to stay up a little longer (his father didn't even say anything about the time), Aunt Elly said, "Okay, let's hear it."

"Hear what?" his father asked innocently.

"Who's the woman who got you out of your tie and bought you that sweater?"

"How do you know *she* bought it?"

"You haven't got such good taste."

His father laughed. "You're awfully curious, aren't you?"

"Of course we're curious, right, Michael?"

"Michael already knows all about her," his father teased.

"*What?* You're kidding!" Aunt Elly shot up in her chair and frowned at Michael. "Nobody ever tells me anything around here. Why didn't you say anything?"

"I didn't get the chance," he grumbled. "I had to do the shopping, set the table, help make supper, and wash the dishes."

Everyone laughed.

Then his father told them the same story Michael had heard that afternoon, but in a lot more detail. He didn't leave out a thing, not even the part about how Michael had run away and was gone the whole night, even though Aunt Elly and Uncle Bob already knew all about that.

"So actually, you've got Michael to thank for meeting Helen," Aunt Elly remarked.

"Yes." He and Michael glanced at each other.

"I think this calls for a drink," said Uncle Bob. "And you, Michael, off to bed. You've got to be up early for practice."

He'd stood up and kissed Aunt Elly and Uncle Bob good night, the way he always did. When he got to his father he didn't quite know what to do with himself; he felt his face turning red.

His father had saved the day by getting up and announcing, "The drinks are on me, Bob. I've got a bottle of Scotch for you in my bag. Sleep well, Michael."

He'd laid his hand on Michael's shoulder and walked him into the hallway, where his suitcase stood.

Michael rolled over on his side, yawning. He listened to the murmur of voices in the room below, and after a while he heard the front door slam. His father was gone. For the first time, Michael wondered when he would see him again.

TWELVE

THE NEXT MORNING MICHAEL COULD HARDLY WAIT FOR JUDITH to arrive. He knew she usually had to drop her brother off at the daycare center before school; she'd probably show up at the last minute.

But when the bell rang, there was still no sign of her.

Mr. Beekman glanced around the classroom. "We seem to be missing Judith," he said.

"Michael misses her, that's for sure," Robert said drily.

Everyone laughed, and Michael couldn't help blushing. Why didn't Robert just mind his own business?

The first hour crawled by. Still no Judith; she must not be coming. Too bad. Now he couldn't tell her about his father. And he couldn't visit her this afternoon either; he had to go to the pool. On Wednesdays he had special practice: "top training," as Mr. Rovers called it. He had to be in the pool by four o'clock, but if he hurried, he might be able to stop over at Judith's on the way there. He'd risk it. He was dying to hear how things had gone with her mother, whether there was money missing from her wallet or not.

While the class was watching a film about China, Michael's thoughts drifted to his father. Parents could be so complicated! Just when he'd finally decided not to have anything more to do with him, he'd shown up again and acted really nice.

Michael still wasn't sure he liked that very much; it made him feel uneasy.

And look at Judith: she was worried sick about her mother. Actually, she was more worried about her mother's boyfriend, who was probably stealing money.

Robert nudged him. "Wanna play soccer this afternoon?" he whispered.

"I've got practice," Michael whispered back.

"Basketball?"

"No, swimming."

Robert sighed. Michael never had time anymore—except for stupid old Judith.

After school, Michael pedaled as fast as he could to get to Judith's house. It was a pretty long way, but he was lucky: all the traffic lights were green. At last he arrived, out of breath, and jumped off his bike. He noticed somebody peeking out from behind the curtains in the first-floor window.

He rang the bell and waited. The woman at the window was still watching him. He rang again. Why didn't Judith answer the door?

Michael took a few steps back and looked up. The windows with the Venetian blinds stared down at him in silence. No sign of life.

Disappointed, he got back on his bike and started off down the block. Just as he reached the corner, an old Renault turned into the street, and when he looked around he saw the car pull up outside Judith's front door. A woman got out and stuck a key in the lock. Judith's mother?

Michael quickly turned around and rode back. The woman's trunk was open, and she was lugging a box of groceries into the house.

Michael slowed down and asked, "Are you Judith's mother?"

The woman frowned; she seemed to be in a hurry. "Yes, why?"

"I'm Michael. I rang the bell a few times, but nobody answered. Would you like me to carry the box upstairs for you?"

"There's no need, I can do it myself."

She'd planted herself in the doorway, as if she were trying to keep him out. She was still holding the heavy box of groceries.

"I'm Michael," he repeated. "I came to see Judith."

"Judith is sick," said her mother.

"She didn't get beaten up again, did she?" Michael asked worriedly.

"Beaten up? What are you talking about?" Her eyes were suddenly filled with suspicion.

"You know. A while ago she got attacked by those kids on the street. They beat her black and blue."

"Oh, that!" cried Judith's mother. "Yes, she was completely hysterical when she came home. Things like that happen around here all the time, and the police do nothing to stop it."

She put the box on the stairs and nervously shoved her hair behind her ears. "Hey listen, I've gotta go upstairs. I'll tell Judith you stopped by."

"But can't I even come and—"

"No, no, she's sleeping. She's got a terrible headache. The excitement wouldn't be good for her."

She gave him a forced smile. "Bye, uh, what did you say your name was?"

"Michael."

"Oh, yes ... okay, bye, Michael."

The door slammed shut.

Judith had recognized Michael's voice instantly. She'd hidden at the top of the stairs and listened to what they were saying. Her knees grew weak with terror when Michael began talking about the boys who'd beaten her up.

When she heard her mother coming up the stairs, she quickly sneaked back to her chair and pretended to be absorbed in a book. Her mother pushed open the door and slammed the box down on the table. She marched up to Judith and snatched the book out of her hands.

"What the hell was that all about?" she shouted. "And who's Michael?"

"A ... a boy from my class."

"And what was he doing here?"

Judith shrugged her shoulders.

"Answer me!"

Judith ducked, but it was too late: the book came crashing down. She covered her head with her arms and cried, "He's just a boy from my class!"

"Has he ever been up here?"

"No ... yes ... ow, Mommy ... don't, don't, please Mommy

... He had to bring me something from the teacher!" she screamed.

The book stopped in midair. "*What* did he bring you, and when?"

"A while ago, when you ... when I had to stay home. You called school and said I was sick. Mr. Beekman asked Michael to bring me a bag of licorice."

"I told you not to answer the door!" screamed her mother.

"I didn't, Mommy, I swear. I just let him ring, like today. But then the phone rang, and I thought it was you, but it was Michael. He called me from the butcher's and told me he was coming over. So then I *had* to answer the door."

Her mother raised her arm again. "And what was that story about a bunch of kids beating you up?"

"Michael asked how I got that bruise on my cheek," said Judith, her voice shaking. "So I told him that I ... that I was attacked by some boys in the street."

"Yes, lying comes easy to you, doesn't it?" her mother jeered. "But you better get this straight: your pal Michael is never to set foot in this house again. Is that clear? I've warned you often enough, I don't want people poking their noses in my business."

"Yes, Mommy," whispered Judith.

"And as far as Nico's concerned, he's coming over for supper tonight, so you can accuse him right to his face."

Judith stared at her in dismay. "Do *I* have to tell him?"

"Of course, who else? You're the one who saw him, aren't you?" her mother sneered. She flung the book down on the table and stormed into the bedroom, where Dennis, who still had a fever, began to cry.

Judith sat there, miserable, and listened to her mother trying to soothe Dennis back to sleep.

Judith kept glancing up at the clock. In half an hour, Nico would arrive. The dull pounding in her head grew steadily worse. She'd spent the whole afternoon worrying what to do about Michael. Her mother must never find out that she went home with him at lunchtime, that was certain, but what could she tell Michael to keep him from coming here?

The day before, when Mommy had beaten her with the rolling pin, she must've knocked her out. Fortunately, because otherwise she probably would've gone on hitting her; now the pain in her back and shoulders wasn't so bad. Just her head ... Judith carefully felt the lump on the back of her head; it was a good thing nobody could see it. Something cold had brought her around again; her mother had splashed water in her face and laid her on the sofa. At first she didn't know where she was; the room looked unfamiliar, and the air was filled with a strange rattling sound that confused her even more.

Slowly it had dawned on her that the rattling was her mother's voice, fragments of which still hung in the air—"Nico ... too much ... alone ... can't take it ... do something ... nobody ..."

Nobody ... That last word had stuck in her mind.

"Say something, Judith, say something!" The sentence traveled down a long tunnel before it reached her eardrums.

She'd struggled to speak; her lips moved, but no sound came out.

"Say something!"

"I'm ... I'm ..." she whispered.

"You're what?" It sounded urgent.

"Nobody ..." she breathed out.

Then she'd heard Dennis calling her name. His little voice came floating toward her and drew her back to her senses.

"Dennis," she'd whispered, and suddenly she realized where she was.

"Oh, Judith ... you had me scared to death." Her mother's eyes were frighteningly large, and filled with tears.

Judith set the table. The pain in her head made her queasy, and her hands were shaking. When the doorbell rang, her mother flew down the stairs; there was laughter in the foyer, and then silence. Now they were kissing, Judith knew it.

She never understood how her mother could change so completely from one minute to the next.

Last night Mommy had been really sweet to her again. She'd pampered her, gone out of her way to make her comfortable. Nothing was too much trouble. She'd bustled nervously around the house, brought out a sleeping bag and pillow and installed Judith on the sofa. When Judith said she wasn't hungry, her mother made soup and urged her to eat. She'd even fed her! And then Judith had felt that hot, burning sensation behind her eyes, the way she always did when her mother was kind to her, and she'd been unable to keep back the tears.

"Does it hurt?" her mother had asked worriedly, and she'd nodded—but *that* wasn't why she was crying.

This morning, too, things had been going fine, until Michael rang the doorbell. After that everything had gone wrong again, but at least she hadn't been beaten. Not hard, anyway.

Dennis began calling her. He'd spent most of the day in bed. Judith hurried into the bedroom. She was glad to have an excuse to get away, so she wouldn't have to sit around with Nico and her mother.

She quickly got out one of his books and began reading to him. But she wasn't really concentrating; she was too busy listening to the sounds in the foyer. After a while she heard footsteps heading up the stairs and Nico's voice echoing in the stairwell.

"So Dennis is sick, huh? Well, I guess we better go in and see how he's doing!"

The bedroom door swung open. "Hey, are you here too, Judith? Reading to your little brother?" Nico had the habit of asking one question after another, without waiting for an answer. "Hey, Dennis, what's this I hear about you being sick? Got the flu? Look, Nico's brought you something. A car. Whaddya think of that?"

"Car," Dennis repeated, holding out his hand.

"You know, Judith, you don't look so good yourself," Nico boomed. "Are you sure you're not coming down with the flu, too?" He ruffled Judith's hair and cried, "Jesus, what's this? A lump as big as a baseball! Can I see it? Hey, Connie, your daughter's got a lump as big as a baseball! Does it hurt? How did you get it?"

"She and Dennis were fooling around yesterday, and she banged her head against a cabinet," her mother answered quickly.

"Wow, that must've been some fall! I'll bet it still hurts. Is that why you're so pale? Maybe this'll help. Here, look, this is for you."

He thrust a roll of licorice into her hands.

"You like licorice, don't you? Enjoy it. And no more of that rough stuff, promise?"

Judith nodded, mumbling, "Thank you, Nico."

But Nico had already turned around and was on his way to the kitchen.

"So, what's for supper? Smells great, baby, almost as good as you, ha ha ... want me to set the table? What? It's already set?"

His voice droned on and on. Judith stood there holding the roll of licorice.

"Me car," Dennis announced as he rode the car back and forth over his pillow.

She watched him dejectedly, then put the roll of licorice on the table next to his bed.

Judith couldn't swallow a bite. No one really noticed, because she was trying to feed Dennis at the same time. Pale and tense, she sat at the table and waited for the moment when she'd have to tell Nico what she'd seen. So far, Nico and her mother had been too involved with each other to pay any attention to her. Nico was telling a story about some funny experience he'd had on his vacation, and they were both roaring with laughter.

Judith felt a wave of nausea, as she often did when she had such a bad headache.

When the laughter had died down, Nico turned to her. "You're really not looking too good, Judith," he said. He seemed genuinely concerned. "You sure you're okay?"

This time, he did wait for an answer.

"I ... I've got a bad headache," Judith stammered, and tears sprang to her eyes. Tears of despair, but also because he was being so nice to her.

"There's always *something* the matter with Judith," her mother snapped.

"It's probably because she banged her head," said Nico.

Judith stared at her plate. "May I be excused?" She looked pleadingly at her mother. "I don't feel very well."

"I'll bet you don't," her mother replied, giving her a meaningful look. "Okay, go on."

Judith stood up and fled to her room.

THIRTEEN

THAT EVENING MICHAEL WAS UNUSUALLY QUIET. HE SAT AT the table in the living room, doing his homework. Uncle Bob was at a meeting, and Aunt Elly was putting the twins to bed. After that she made coffee and flopped down on the sofa.

"At last, time for myself." She sighed and kicked off her shoes.

Michael glanced at her. He was gnawing his pen, and his aunt recognized that "I want to talk to you, but you've gotta go first" look.

"You must have a lot on your mind," she began gently.

Michael nodded.

"Your father?"

"Yeah, that's part of it."

"He's really changed, he's more like he used to be, when your mother was alive."

"Did you know him well in those days?"

"Yes, pretty well, though your father's always been a very closed person. But that never bothered your mother. Somehow she was always able to get through to him, and I have the feeling that Helen knows how to get through to him, too. Can you still remember her?"

"Yes, better than my own mother, even, and I've only met Helen once."

"You were awfully young when your mother died."

"What was she like?"

Michael had asked that question more than once in the past few years, and Aunt Elly had always told him what he wanted to know. He never minded if she repeated things, because the more often he heard her memories of his mother, the more they became his own.

Aunt Elly drew up her legs and made herself comfortable. "Your mother?" she asked. That's how she always began.

"Yes. Was she like you?"

"In some ways. We both knew how to handle your father, for instance, except that he and I used to argue a lot. Your mother got along with him better because she was more flexible, more tactful. She also had more patience ..."

"You're pretty patient yourself," said Michael.

"Thanks, honey." Aunt Elly smiled. "Your mother had lots of boyfriends," she went on, "but she chose the most difficult one: your dad. He was somewhat older than the others, and next to him, they all seemed very young and inexperienced. Your father had brains, too. He was so smart, he could talk circles around everybody. It used to make me nervous, but not your mother. She wasn't at all impressed. She thought it was convenient, though. 'He's a walking dictionary,' she used to say, 'I hardly ever have to look anything up anymore. The only word he has trouble with is "affection," but I'm working on that.' And then she'd start kissing him, right in front of everybody. You should've seen his face; he never knew where to look—your mother was a pretty enthusiastic kisser," said Aunt Elly, laughing.

"Just like you," teased Michael.

"Yes, but fortunately, Uncle Bob doesn't mind."

"He sure doesn't." Now Michael was laughing too. He thought of the plumber who had walked into the kitchen the week before, just as Aunt Elly was kissing Uncle Bob goodbye. "Well, I can see I don't have to wish *you* two a good morning," he'd said. "You're already having one!"

"But the truth is," Aunt Elly went on, "your parents were crazy about each other. You know, when I think about it, your father must've gone to pieces when your mother died—he just didn't show it. He dealt with it in his own way, by being extra hard on himself, and on you, too. He probably thought that was the best way to cope, but he wasn't aware of the harm it was doing to you. He may have been smart, but there were some things he didn't understand. It took years for him to get the message, but by that time he'd pretty much accepted your mother's death. I think Helen's had a good influence on him, too. I haven't seen him that relaxed in years. You know what he said last night, for the very first time, after you'd gone to bed? He said, 'The best thing I ever did for Michael was to send him to you.' That's not what he's always said. He sometimes used to give us the feeling that we'd stolen you from him."

Michael chewed thoughtfully on his pen. "He was acting differently to me, too, but I kind of have to get used to it. I feel like I hardly know him."

"That's because you still have a certain image of him, from the old days, when you lived in America. But parents can change too, you know."

Michael wiggled his foot nervously. "You're not going to send me back, are you? I mean ... if he marries Helen or something."

"Are you kidding?" Aunt Elly exclaimed. "Not a chance! Only if you want to go back; it's totally up to you."

Michael heaved a sigh of relief. "That's what Dad said, too. He also said he'd like it if I spent my vacation there sometime, but I don't think that's such a good idea."

"I do," said Aunt Elly.

"You mean you *want* me to go?" Michael asked, confused.

"No, *I* want to go!" Aunt Elly laughed. "I think we should all go. A couple of weeks in America sounds like fun."

"You mean you'd all come with me?" cried Michael. "Wow, that'd be great!"

"Hey, didn't you have homework to do?" asked Aunt Elly.

"Not that much." Michael hesitated, opened his mouth and closed it again.

Aunt Elly looked at him questioningly. "Is there something else on your mind?"

"Yes. I met Judith's mother today," he blurted out.

"What was she like?"

"Weird. I don't know how to explain it. She wouldn't even let me in."

"Why not?"

"I don't know. Judith was sick again, so I thought I'd stop by and ask how things had turned out with her mother's boyfriend."

Michael told her the story of the missing money, and what Judith had seen.

"What a terrible situation," said Aunt Elly sympathetically, "for Judith *and* her mother."

"Yeah." Michael frowned. "But the weirdest thing was that she didn't even know who I was. She asked me my name, and when I told her I was Michael, she acted like she'd never heard the name before. She must know I've been riding home with Judith almost every day since she got attacked, and about Judith coming here. Don't you think?"

Now even Aunt Elly seemed surprised. "Maybe she's just a little overworked. From what I understand, she has to support the whole family. I think Judith must be overworked, too. She looks so pale, as if she hasn't been getting enough sleep."

"She has to help her mother around the house, and take care of her little brother, too."

"Yes, she told me. It's no wonder she's sick all the time. You really like Judith, don't you?"

Michael nodded. "She reminds me a lot of Steffie, the girl who lived next door to us before we moved to Washington, the one I told you about. But she's also very different. Judith is much ... much more quiet, but not boring or anything. And she always gives you the feeling ..."—Michael wriggled shyly in his chair—"that she needs you."

"I think she does." Aunt Elly smiled at him. "I think you mean a lot to her."

"Really?"

"Yes."

Then why doesn't her mother know anything about me? a little voice nagged in Michael's head.

FOURTEEN

"GOOD TO HAVE YOU BACK," MR. BEEKMAN SAID TO JUDITH. "Would you mind staying in class for a while during recess? I'd like to talk to you."

"Yes, sir." Embarrassed, Judith went to her seat. What did he want? In a few weeks they'd be getting their Easter report cards; maybe hers was very bad.

She glanced anxiously around the room. Michael's seat was empty.

"Hey, Michael's not here," said Mr. Beekman, surprised. "Does anyone know where he is?"

"Yeah, Judith does!" cried Diana.

Everyone looked at Judith, who turned bright red. She heard smothered giggles.

"Selma's absent, too," Mr. Beekman went on, as if he hadn't heard a thing.

"Selma's got the flu," somebody called out.

The class began. Judith struggled through the first two hours. She really tried to concentrate. Mr. Beekman saw her tense little face bent over her reading workbook. He walked around the classroom, stopping here and there to explain something. When he reached Judith's desk, he lay his hand on her shoulder. She cringed.

"Did I scare you?" he asked.

"Yes, Mr. Beekman," Judith mumbled. She listened to his footsteps as he walked away; her heart beat like a drum. Why did she have to act like such a baby? Her palms were clammy, and she was trembling so hard she could barely hold the pen.

The bell rang, and immediately the air was filled with stumbling, screaming, and shuffling.

"Are you coming?" asked Diana.

"In a minute," said Judith. "I've got to finish something first."

"Oh, forget it." Diana spun around indignantly and marched out of the room.

Mr. Beekman was standing at the door. When everyone had gone, he said, "So, now we can talk in peace."

He sat down at his desk and motioned to her to pull up a chair. Then he took out two apples and calmly began peeling them. He offered her a piece, and put one in his mouth.

As he went on peeling, he said, "You know, Judith, you've been absent quite a lot these past few months. Your mother wrote that you've been having very bad headaches."

"Yes. I had a concussion once," Judith said timidly.

"Oh, what a shame. How did it happen?"

"I ... I fell down the stairs."

"At home?"

Judith nodded.

"Oh, no, I mean my aunt's house," she quickly corrected herself. "And after that I started getting all those headaches."

"That's too bad," said Mr. Beekman sympathetically. "By the way, before I forget, what was the name of your old school?"

"The Margriet School."

"Here in town?"

"Yes." Judith told him which neighborhood. "And before that I went to St. Joseph's."

"You've been to quite a few different schools," her teacher observed. He handed her another piece of apple.

Judith nodded.

"Why is that?"

"Because my mother got a new job."

Judith began to feel more confident. This had nothing to do with her report card; Mr. Beekman just wanted to know which schools she'd been to.

"And once because Uncle Ben came to live with us—he's Dennis's father, my little brother. Our house was too small, so we moved to an apartment. But when Uncle Ben went away, the apartment was too expensive for us, so we had to find another place to live."

Her teacher nodded. "What about your own father?"

Judith shrugged her shoulders. "My parents got divorced when I was a baby."

"So your mother's all on her own."

Judith nodded.

"And you must have to help out around the house. Take your brother to daycare, pick him up, do the shopping ..."

"My mother usually does the shopping," Judith told him, "but I pick up my brother, and I take care of him until my mother gets home."

"That's a big job," said Mr. Beekman. "I'm impressed."

Judith glowed. "Aw, he's not too much trouble," she said. "Only sometimes."

Her teacher smiled.

"But I'll bet you do a lot more than just take care of your brother. And there's your homework, on top of everything else. I think it's quite an achievement. For your mother, too. I'm sure she's got a very busy life: a job, two children to raise—that's no easy task."

Judith nodded. She was feeling almost completely at ease.

"I just want you to know, you mustn't ever hesitate to ask me for help. That's what I'm here for."

"With homework, you mean?" asked Judith. Without thinking, she rolled up her sleeves.

"I mean with everything. You can trust me, Judith. If there's something on your mind, you can always talk to me about it. You seem to me like a very serious girl, with a big sense of responsibility. But everybody needs someone to talk to now and then. I may be your teacher, but I'm not such a bad guy. You can always come to me."

He gave her a nod of encouragement. "This last piece is for you," he said.

Judith took the slice of apple and put it in her mouth.

"Hey, where did you get all those bruises?" Mr. Beekman asked, grabbing hold of her arm.

He felt her stiffen. Then she quickly pulled back her arm and started rolling down her sleeves. "Oh, my brother and I were playing around, and I bumped into a cabinet," she explained with her mouth full. She avoided his eyes.

"It looks to me like you two had more of a boxing match." Mr. Beekman pushed back his chair. "Come on, let's go join the others," he said.

They walked out of the classroom together. When they

got outside she blinked, and her eyes filled with tears. Why did she always have to start blubbering every time somebody was nice to her?

At lunchtime Judith jumped on her bike and hurried to Michael's house. She'd been wondering all morning whether or not she should go, but as soon as the bell rang, she raced to the bicycle rack.

When she got to his house, she was all out of breath. She walked around the back, the way she always did, and leaned her bike against the shed. But the twins didn't come running out to greet her, and when she walked into the kitchen she didn't see anyone, either.

"Hello! Anybody home?" she called out.

"Is that you, Judith?" came Aunt Elly's voice from upstairs. "I'll be right down!" Moments later she was standing before her, with Michele in her arms.

"Feeling better?" Aunt Elly gave Judith a kiss, the way she always did with Michael. Judith still felt slightly uncomfortable when Aunt Elly kissed her or stroked her hair.

"You still look a bit pale," said Aunt Elly. "But I'm glad you're here, because now Michael's sick. He's in a lousy mood. He's got a sore throat, so I thought I'd better keep him home today, despite his protests! Why don't you go up and see him? I'll bring you both some soup."

Judith leaned down to hug Michele. "Bichael sick," Michele told her, "but Bichele not sick. Bichele better."

"Michele hasn't even *been* sick," said Aunt Elly with a laugh.

"Where are David and Frank?"

"They're having lunch at a friend's house, but if they'd known you were coming, I'm sure they never would've gone. They've really missed you," said Aunt Elly warmly. "You know the way to Michael's room, don't you?"

"Oh yes!" Judith was already halfway up the stairs. She gave a quick knock on Michael's door and then walked right in.

"Hey, it's you!" Michael sat up in bed, smiling weakly. He looked feverish, and his eyes didn't have their usual twinkle.

"I'm so pissed off," he complained. "I wasn't even allowed to go to practice this morning."

"Poor thing," Judith teased. "How's your throat?"

"Oh, it's fine," said Michael optimistically, but Judith could see he was having trouble swallowing. "What about you? Are you all better?"

"Yes."

"I went by your house," Michael told her. "I stood there ringing the bell, like a real idiot, but you didn't answer. Just as I was leaving, your mother drove up, and she said you were asleep."

"I was," Judith lied. "My mother told me later that she'd seen you."

There was a silence. Neither of them looked at the other. Feeling awkward, Judith got up and went to the dresser, where the koala bear stood. Strange, thought Michael, she never touches things. She just looks.

"You can hold him if you want," he said. "He won't break."

Judith carefully picked him up and sat back down on the bed.

"You know what I like best about him?"

"What?" asked Michael.

"He's getting bald. His fur's wearing off."

"Why do you like that so much?"

"That's how I can tell he's your favorite bear."

"He was Steffie's favorite bear, too," said Michael.

"I know, you told me."

There was another silence. Judith gazed at the bear and fiddled with its one remaining ear; the other was gone.

"Hey, whatever happened with your mom's money?" Michael sat straight up in bed, propped himself up against his pillow, and wrapped his arms around his knees.

"Oh, everything turned out fine," Judith answered, trying to sound casual. "There was nothing missing, thank goodness. Nico was probably just looking for a cigarette." Judith kept her eyes on the bear.

"So you did all that worrying for nothing."

"Yes. Pretty stupid, wasn't it?"

"You know what I think is stupid?" Michael blurted out. "That your mother didn't even know who I was." He sounded hurt.

Judith's fingers tightened around the bear. "No, she doesn't," she confessed unhappily. "You're a secret."

"A secret? What do you mean?" Michael frowned.

"She doesn't like it when people come over." Judith broke out in a sweat.

"Why not?"

"She's always afraid something might happen. To Dennis, or me. She's ... She worries a lot ..."

"Does that mean she doesn't know about you coming here at lunchtime?"

"No, she doesn't know about that either," said Judith in a quavering voice. "I haven't told her, because I know she'll just worry."

"This is all so complicated," said Michael, thinking out loud. "Why would she worry about you coming to my house?"

Judith shrugged helplessly. "Promise you won't tell anyone?" she asked.

"That's one thing you don't have to worry about," Michael reassured her. "But you know what I think is weird?"

"What?" Judith waited anxiously.

"A few weeks ago, you got bashed up by those creeps. That was because you were alone. Your mother shouldn't be scared, she should be *glad* somebody's bicycling home with you."

"I don't get it either," Judith admitted.

"Parents can be pretty confusing sometimes." Michael sighed. "Take my father, for instance. He was just here visiting."

Judith was relieved that her mother was no longer the topic of conversation. "How was it?"

"Incredible."

Judith looked at him in surprise.

"It was almost *fun*," said Michael, chuckling. He told Judith about his father's visit to the swimming pool, and their talk in the coffee shop, where his father had told him how he'd bumped into Helen again, the gym teacher who'd found him asleep in her car when he'd run away from home.

"And now they're going out!" Michael got so excited he started coughing. "He was really different, didn't keep putting me down like he used to. You know what he actually said? 'There must've been times when you really hated me, and I can't say I blame you.' *My* father! I reminded him how he always used to say that sports weren't important, and he said, 'Yes, that was stupid of me.' He thought it was 'shortsighted,' that's what he said. Can you believe it? And he's even started jogging!"

Michael was coughing and laughing at the same time.

"It's all because of Helen, you know. She's a gym teacher. She makes him run his legs off!"

Just then Aunt Elly came in with two steaming mugs of soup.

"Well, I can see your spirits have risen," she said, smiling. "Your temperature too, I'll bet." She laid her hand on his forehead. "I was right, you're burning up."

"Don't tell me I have to stay home again tomorrow!"

"Judith, help!" Aunt Elly begged. "Is this boy sick, or isn't he?"

"Yes."

"Thanks a lot," Michael grumbled.

Judith looked at the clock and cried, "Oh no! I've gotta hurry, or I'll be late for school!"

"But you haven't eaten your sandwich yet," said Aunt Elly.

"I'll eat on my bike." She took a few sips of the hot soup and zipped up her jacket.

"Can you come back tomorrow?"

"Only if you're sick," said Judith.

"That means yes," said Aunt Elly. "Come on, Judith, honey, I'll walk you to the door."

FIFTEEN

THAT SAME AFTERNOON JUDITH'S TEACHER CALLED THE MARGRIET School. The phone was answered after the first ring.

"Margriet School, Evelien de Bruin speaking."

"Good afternoon. This is Arno Beekman from Cloverleaf Elementary School. I'm calling for information about one of your former pupils, Judith Van Gelder. She's been in my class since the beginning of January."

"Judith Van Gelder?" repeated the woman on the other end. "Yes, I remember her. She attended the Margriet School for about a year and a half. I even had her in my class for several months. A quiet little girl, rather pale and thin, kept to herself most of the time," Evelien de Bruin summed up. "Oh yes, and there was always something wrong with her. One week she'd have the flu, the next week it was a headache, which meant she had to miss gym. Swimming was also a problem, because she had some sort of rash."

"Sounds familiar. Have you ever met her mother?"

"No. She never came to Parents' Night—the year before, either. I once phoned her and she promised to come. She sounded very concerned about her daughter. She told me that Judith had always been a sickly child, ever since she was a baby. That's probably why she was always so warmly dressed. Even when it was sweltering outside, she'd still be wearing a turtleneck sweater. The other children used to tease her about it."

"You know, now that you mention it ..." said Mr. Beekman thoughtfully. "Let me ask you, was she able to keep up with the rest of the class?"

"With great difficulty, though I did get the impression that she was doing her best. But she never asked any questions, and since she was so quiet, you had to be careful not to overlook her."

"I know what you mean. Did she have any friends?"

"No ... no, I don't think she did—at least, no best friend, the way girls often do at that age. She never quite seemed to fit in. Actually, I felt rather sorry for her. Though she never acted pitiful, not at all. Not even the time she was attacked by a gang of boys. They beat her up very badly. The poor child was covered with bruises, but she behaved like a true stoic."

Mr. Beekman frowned. He thought of the bruises on her arm. That couldn't have been ...

"And how is Judith these days?"

"Hard to say. She's still absent a lot, as I've already told you. But fortunately there's a boy in the class whom she's been spending time with."

"It sounds to me as if she's doing very well! Tell me, Mr. Beekman, what was the reason for your call?"

"I'm not so sure myself." He paused. "Perhaps it's because she always tries so hard not to attract any attention. As if she wanted to be ... invisible. I just find it strange. Listen, I hope I haven't taken up too much of your time."

"Not at all," said Evelien de Bruin warmly. "I appreciate your concern for the child."

They exchanged a few more words and then hung up.

Mr. Beekman scratched himself behind the ear. "Well, that wasn't much help," he said out loud. "But what was I expecting?"

When Judith arrived at the daycare center that afternoon, she was told that her mother had already picked up Dennis.

Surprised and slightly worried, she cycled home as fast as she could. Just as she was putting her key in the door, a pale hand pushed aside the curtain in the first-floor window. Judith gave a quick wave, and the hand waved stiffly back.

As she hurried up the stairs, she heard voices and laughter coming from the living room. They hardly ever had guests. Who could it be? Not Nico, anyway: it was a woman's voice.

She took off her jacket and walked hesitantly into the living room. The conversation stopped, and her mother cried: "Look who's here! It's Judith! You probably don't even recognize her." She put her arm around Judith's shoulder and pushed her toward the sofa. "This is Aunt Ria, from Canada. She's moving back to Holland."

Judith smiled shyly at the small, plump woman, who looked nothing like her mother.

Aunt Ria hugged her tightly and exclaimed, "It's unbelievable! She's the spitting image ..." She took Judith's face in her hands and kissed her loudly on the cheeks. Even her kisses sounded plump. "The spitting image," she repeated, pulling Judith down beside her on the sofa. "I can't believe how much you look—"

Her mother's face darkened, and she interrupted Aunt Ria to ask if she wanted more tea.

"Oh yes, please."

Judith's mother got up and went into the kitchen, Dennis close behind her. There was the sound of water running, a kettle being filled.

"The last time I saw you, Judith, you were three years old," Aunt Ria went on. "You and your mom lived in Schiedam. Do you remember that?"

Judith shook her head.

"Unbelievable," sighed Aunt Ria, gazing at her. "You look so much like—"

Judith's mother poked her head around the door. "Judith, dear, why don't you go upstairs and put on another sweater?" Judith couldn't help hearing the tension in her voice.

She did what she was told, but the moment she left the room she heard her mother shouting, "Why did you have to bring that up? You only just got here, and already you're—"

"But it's true, that child looks exactly—"

"Do you think I *like* that?" her mother shrieked.

Judith stopped, and pricked up her ears.

"Does that still bother you, after all this time?" Aunt Ria asked gently. "You couldn't do anything about it, Connie. Nobody could."

"Don't you think I know that! But Mama never stopped blaming me, did she? You were there, you know what I'm talking about. It was never a problem for you, but for me ... me ..." Judith's mother began stuttering. "She ignored me, till the day she died. I just didn't exist anymore, as far as she was concerned. No matter what I did. You were the only one who stood up for me."

"Except when you got married. I warned you about that. But you wouldn't listen. The only reason you married that man was to get back at Mama."

"And it didn't even work!" her mother cried bitterly.

Judith tiptoed up the stairs. Who? Who did she look like? Grandma? Mommy hardly ever talked about the past. "The past is dead," her mother always said. Though she did talk about Aunt Ria now and again.

Judith opened the door of her closet. She knew the sweater was just an excuse to get her out of the room. She decided to put on the red one, the one Mommy had bought her a while back. The strange thing was, Mommy never let her wear it; she probably thought it was too good to wear to school. But Judith was sure she wouldn't mind if she wore it for Aunt Ria.

She slipped it over her head. She had to hurry; Mommy might get impatient if she stayed away too long. She ran a comb through her hair and tied it back with a rubber band, the way her mother often did. Then she ran back downstairs.

"Is this better?" she asked, looking expectantly at her mother, who was still talking to Aunt Ria. Both heads turned. On her aunt's round, pink face was a look of dismay. Her mother froze. Then she got up and started coming toward her. Judith backed away in terror, and bumped into the little table where Aunt Ria had put her teacup. The table wobbled, the teacup fell and broke.

"Get upstairs," her mother hissed, "and stay there."

Judith fled from the room. She thought she'd be making Mommy happy by putting on the sweater, and now everything was ruined because of that stupid cup.

Judith's mother picked up the pieces, her hands shaking.

"She can't help it," said Aunt Ria quietly.

"Neither can I," muttered Judith's mother. "Neither can I." She looked down and saw that she'd cut herself.

Aunt Ria got up from the sofa, clicked open her pocket-book, and took out a handkerchief, which she wrapped around the bleeding finger.

"Poor little buttercup," she said. Her voice was filled with sympathy.

"That's what you always used to say when we were kids."

Aunt Ria put her arms around her and held her tightly.

"I'm so glad you're back," said Judith's mother after a while.

"Me too," said Aunt Ria.

SIXTEEN

JUDITH COULD TELL, BY THE SOUND OF THE FOOTSTEPS, THAT Aunt Ria was coming up the stairs. Moments later the door opened, and she walked into the room, panting.

"Whew! I didn't think I'd make it. Give me a minute to catch my breath, sweetie," she gasped, and sank down next to Judith on the bed.

"Every time I sit down somewhere, it either squeaks, cracks, or groans," she told her. "Once a chair collapsed right under me, and the whole house shook."

When she saw that Judith was laughing too, she put her arm around her and drew her close.

"You know, it's just not fair," she said. "Your mother has two children and no husband, and I have a husband and no children. I would've loved to have a daughter like you."

Judith couldn't believe her ears. Aunt Ria's words made her feel happy and shy at the same time.

"Your mother's gone out shopping. Don't worry about the teacup, Judith, it could happen to anybody. Your mom's not quite herself, with me here and all. Neither am I, in fact. We haven't seen each other for such a long time."

Judith picked at the red sweater. There was something she was dying to ask, but she didn't dare.

"The last time I saw you, you were a little girl. Actually, you're still kind of small for your age. Anyway, that was before Dennis was born."

"Are you staying with us for long?" Judith sounded so hopeful that Aunt Ria gave her a squeeze.

"A week. Then I'm going to Utrecht, to visit some cousins of Uncle Chris. I've got to start looking for a place for us to live. Uncle Chris will be arriving in about a month, and I'd like to have found something by then."

"A whole week? Great!" Judith beamed. "You can sleep in my bed if you want. I'll sleep on the floor. I don't mind. Really!"

"Your mother said something about a sofa bed in the living room, but I think it would be much more fun sleeping with you. Though I must say, it's pretty chilly up here." Aunt Ria looked around the room. "Don't you have any heating?"

"No."

"But isn't it cold in the winter?"

"Aw, you get used to it," said Judith.

"In Canada it can get really cold. Sometimes twenty or thirty degrees below zero! That's why they built this huge underground shopping center in Montreal. You can spend all day there if you like. They've got movie theaters, restaurants, everything you can imagine. And it's nice and warm, all winter long."

Downstairs, they heard a door slam.

"I think your mommy's home. Are you coming down?"

Judith looked at her anxiously. "But I promised to stay upstairs."

"You're not planning on sitting up here all by yourself, are you? I see so little of you as it is. Come on, we'll go down together. I'll explain it to your mom. But you'll have to help me up first!"

Judith was only too happy to do so.

Judith couldn't remember when she'd had such a wonderful afternoon. Aunt Ria told them all about Canada. Her stories were often funny, and the best part, thought Judith, was that Aunt Ria laughed too, as if she were reliving the events. Her laughter was rich and warm, and so contagious that everyone joined in. Even Dennis, though he didn't understand a word of what she was saying.

The happy mood was nearly spoiled when Aunt Ria suggested she sleep in Judith's room.

"No need," said her mother. "You can sleep down here on the sofa bed. It's warmer, too."

"Oh, I'm used to the cold, living in Canada all these years," Aunt Ria said lightly.

"But there's only one bed."

"Please, Mommy?" Judith begged. "I can sleep on the floor. We have an air mattress, don't we?"

"I'd sleep on the sofa if I were you," her mother warned

Aunt Ria. "Judith's been wetting her bed lately."

Judith turned bright red and stared at her plate. She felt the tears coming on; if only she could run away and hide ...

Aunt Ria took Judith's hand and pressed it firmly.

"I'm glad I'm not the only one. I went through a phase like that. I was about ten or eleven, and every night it was the same old thing. Father came up with a solution. He called it the alarm clock trick. I set my alarm to go off every two hours, and then I'd get up and go to the bathroom. After a while it was every three hours, then every four, and in the end I could sleep through the night without wetting my bed. Apparently it's very common. I've got a friend in Toronto with three kids, a boy and twin girls ..."

And then she launched into a story about the twins, both of whom wet their beds almost every night. Aunt Ria told their mother about the alarm clock trick. It helped, but the eight-year-old son was so jealous that his little sisters were allowed to get out of bed every few hours, and were even allowed to read for a while if they couldn't get back to sleep, that he marched into his parents' room one morning and proudly announced that he'd finally wet his bed, and that now he, too, could read at night.

Aunt Ria bubbled with laughter.

"But you won't sleep a wink if the alarm goes off every two hours," Judith's mother persisted.

"I can sleep through anything," Aunt Ria assured her, giving Judith's hand another squeeze.

After supper, Mommy and Aunt Ria put Dennis to bed, while Judith quickly cleared the table and did the dishes.

"What a helpful daughter you've got!" cried Aunt Ria when she came into the kitchen. "Everything's spotless!"

Her mother made no nasty remarks; in fact, she didn't say anything nasty for the rest of the evening.

Judith sat down at the table to do her homework, while Mommy and Aunt Ria chattered away on the sofa.

"Are we bothering you, sweetie?" Aunt Ria asked her every now and then.

Judith shook her head vehemently. Bothering her? Not in a million years ...

"Judith ... Judith ..." She was awakened by Aunt Ria's whispering voice, and sat up on her mattress, still half asleep.

"Come on, I'll help you," said Aunt Ria softly. Suddenly Judith remembered what she had to do. She got up and went downstairs to the bathroom. When she returned, Aunt Ria was already in bed; she'd left the lamp on.

"I've put the alarm clock under your pillow," Aunt Ria told her. "It's set to go off in two hours."

Judith moved the air mattress a little closer to the bed, and crawled into her sleeping bag.

"I'm so glad you're here," she whispered.

"Me too," said Aunt Ria, "and as soon as I've found a house, I want you to come stay with us for a few days."

She switched off the lamp, and in the darkness Judith heard the bed creak.

"Aunt Ria?"

"Mmm ..."

"Can I ask you something?"

The bed creaked again.

"Who do I look like?"

There was a silence.

"I knew you were going to ask me that. You look like Dicky."

"Mommy's brother?"

"And mine," said Aunt Ria.

"He died very young, didn't he?"

"Yes, he was only nine. He fell through the ice. Hasn't Mommy ever told you about that?"

"No ... or maybe she did, I don't remember. Maybe I heard her talking about it to Uncle Ben."

"Dennis's father?"

"Yes."

"Do you ever see him?"

"Only when he comes to pick up Dennis, but that's not very often. Didn't Mommy like Dicky?" The question was out before she knew it.

"Why do you ask?"

"No reason." Judith was glad it was dark.

"No, Dicky was a sweet little boy. Everyone was crazy about him, especially Mama. She never got over his death; it totally changed her."

"What do you mean, changed?"

"Well, the way she treated your mother, for instance. Those two had never gotten along. They were always at each other's throats. Mama wasn't the easiest person, I'll have to admit, but neither was Connie. Actually, they were very much alike, those two, both stubborn and pigheaded, and I guess they clashed. Father was always hushing them up, but once he was gone, they stopped holding it in. It was no fun having to live with them, I can tell you. I myself never had much trouble with Mama, and Dicky ... Dicky was the apple of her eye. She treated him like a little prince, and Connie couldn't stand that."

Aunt Ria turned over; the springs groaned.

"Connie, your mother, felt very neglected. She demanded as much attention from Mama as Dicky did—maybe more. But the only time she ever got it was when they were fighting, and *that* wasn't the kind of attention she needed."

Aunt Ria sighed. "Those fights, those terrible fights ... I hated them. When Mama got mad enough, she'd lose control and start hitting Connie. Hard. She'd never dream of hitting Dicky or me, but your mother made her furious. And what do you think your mom did? She hit right back, just as hard! And then she'd get punished, of course, because you weren't allowed to hit your own mother. She'd have to stay in her room for hours, or go to bed without supper. Usually I'd smuggle something up to her, because I felt so sorry for her. But then came that day in winter ..."

Aunt Ria sighed again.

"It had been very cold, the lake had frozen over, and Dicky wanted to go skating. Mama had the flu. Otherwise she would've gone with him. She told your mother to take him, but Connie wanted to go to her friend's house. I wasn't home that day, but I can just imagine how it went. First a fight, of course, the two of them screaming and cursing, and Dicky waiting patiently in the doorway, holding his ice skates. Your mom gave in in the end, but she was mad as a hornet. 'Be careful,' Mama warned her as they were leaving. 'No!' your mother yelled back.

"First they stopped over at her friend's house to tell her Dicky wanted to go skating on the lake. 'Okay, I'll come too,' said her friend, and it looked like maybe it wasn't going to be such a bad afternoon after all. They had a great time, the three of them. Dicky was a good skater, and proud of it. At one point they decided to have a race. Dicky was way ahead of the other two, but suddenly he fell through a hole in the ice and disappeared ... Your mother tried everything, she yelled and screamed for help, but by the time someone arrived, it was too late. I don't have to tell you what a shock it was for her, for all of us ..."

She paused.

"As I said before, Mama never got over it, and the worst part was, she held Connie responsible for Dicky's death. That was too much for your mother to bear; she felt guilty enough already. The situation got worse and worse, though they weren't actually fighting anymore. Mama had stopped screaming and cursing, she'd found a much better weapon: she ignored Connie, acted as if she didn't even exist. Connie tried everything she could to get into her favor, but when that didn't work, she went on the offensive. One of the things she did was marry a boy who lived on our street, a boy who Mama had always said was a good-for-nothing. Connie married him just to spite her. But it wasn't long before he ran out and left her with you."

Judith had been lying there so quietly, listening, that Aunt Ria asked, "Are you asleep?"

"No ... no ..."

"Maybe I shouldn't be telling you all this."

"I'm glad I know," said Judith softly.

"When you came down this afternoon in that red sweater, and your hair in a ponytail ... you looked so much like Dicky, it was scary. He had beautiful blond hair, too, just like you, and on that last afternoon, on the ice, he was wearing a red sweater. He always looked so good in red."

Judith shuddered. Mommy had given her that red sweater, but she was never allowed to wear it. Now she understood why.

"Did they ... did they ever make up, Mommy and her mother?"

"No ... never. Mama died when you were about two years old. Your mother didn't even go to the funeral. I've never understood how people could let things get that far. But as I said before, those two were very much alike. Stubborn as mules."

She fell silent.

"Am I ... am I like Dicky in any other way?" Judith asked hesitantly.

The bed creaked loudly. Judith felt Aunt Ria's soft hand on her cheek.

"Dicky was a sweet, sensitive little fellow. You couldn't help loving him. In that way, yes, you are like him, but you're not Dicky. You're Judith, and don't ever forget that."

Judith clasped Aunt Ria's hand and held it tightly.

"We better get some sleep," whispered Aunt Ria, "or you'll be all tired out in the morning."

"Okay," Judith whispered back. She rolled over onto her side, but it was a long time before she could fall asleep.

SEVENTEEN

JUDITH PEDALED CHEERFULLY TO SCHOOL. SHE BREATHED deeply; spring was in the air, the sky was a transparent shade of blue, and the trees were just starting to blossom. When she arrived at school she saw Diana at the gate, talking to a group of children. She could tell by the tone of her voice that something was wrong.

"Mr. Beekman's not coming in today," Robert told her. "His father's in the hospital."

"That's too bad. Does that mean we have to go home?"

"We don't know yet."

As they all swarmed into the corridor, Judith looked around for Michael. He wasn't there either.

Mr. Dijkstra, the principal, was waiting for them at the door of the classroom.

"I'll be filling in for Mr. Beekman this morning," he told them. "He should be here later on."

The first few hours passed smoothly. At the end of the morning, just before lunch, Mr. Beekman walked in. He looked tired but relieved.

"What a night!" he said. "My father had to have an emergency bypass, but he seems to be doing pretty well now."

Everyone wanted to know all about it, so Mr. Beekman drew a heart on the blackboard and explained to them exactly what had happened. The class was impressed.

"You didn't sleep the whole night?" asked Karel.

"Not a wink," admitted Mr. Beekman.

"You can take a nap now if you want," Robert called out. "We'll be quiet."

Mr. Beekman laughed. "To tell you the truth, I'm not really in the mood to teach. Why don't you all take out a book, and I'll go get a cup of coffee, to keep me awake."

Michael could hardly wait for Judith to arrive. Time always seemed to go so slowly when you were waiting for somebody! He kept glancing at his watch.

"Finally!" he groaned when Judith walked into the room.

"I ... I pedaled like crazy," she panted. "But I had to stop for every single traffic light." She unzipped her jacket, tossed it on his bed and flopped into a chair.

Michael had to laugh. This wasn't at all like Judith.

"What's up with you?" he asked.

"My aunt's here," she told him. "Aunt Ria. She used to live in Canada, but she's moving back to Holland. She's staying with us for a week."

It was the first time he'd ever heard her talk about her family.

"And this morning Mr. Beekman didn't come in," she went on. "He came later, because his father had a heart operation."

Judith chattered away: about Montreal, where her aunt lived with Uncle Chris, whom she couldn't remember very well, only that he had big feet. And Aunt Ria was very fat but really nice, and they were looking for a house in Utrecht and she could come stay with them for a few days, Aunt Ria had promised. Judith rattled on and on, and didn't even notice that Michael wasn't saying anything.

"So how are *you*?" she finally asked. "Still got a temperature?"

"No," he grumbled. "But Aunt Elly won't let me go back to school yet. Really stupid." Then he fell silent.

Judith began eating her sandwich. When Michael still didn't say anything, she asked, "Is something wrong?"

He shrugged his shoulders and stared straight ahead.

"That means yes," Judith said with her mouth full.

"You seem almost glad I wasn't at school."

"What makes you think *that*?" Judith asked, surprised.

"You're never usually this talkative."

"That's because of Aunt Ria, I think," said Judith. "She's the nicest aunt I know. Except for your aunt, that is."

Michael sulked.

"But school's pretty boring without you there, that's for sure."

"Really?" All of a sudden Michael looked bashful.

Judith nodded, and felt herself blushing. She got up and

went over to the dresser where the koala bear stood.

"I think it's boring without you, too," he confessed. "You're the nicest girl I know."

He watched her as she carefully picked up the little bear. She was standing with her back to him.

"You only think that because I look like Steffie," she said, without turning around.

"That was in the beginning, before I got to know you. But you're not Steffie, you're Judith."

Judith turned around to face him. She had a strange look in her eyes.

"Yes, I'm Judith," she repeated slowly, as if she were hearing her name for the first time. "Judith."

Then, very carefully, she put the bear back on top of the dresser.

The following week passed much too quickly. Judith wished she could hang on to the days, to keep them from slipping away. With Aunt Ria around, the whole house felt like springtime. Even Mommy seemed different. Judith had never seen her looking so happy.

One afternoon when she got out of school, Aunt Ria was waiting for her at the gate.

Mr. Beekman watched as Judith ran up and hugged her. Was that Judith's mother? Maybe now would be a good time to try and make an appointment ... Too late, they were already walking away. Just as he was about to turn around, he saw Michael going with them. Mr. Beekman sighed. With his father in the hospital, Judith had somehow gotten pushed to the back of his mind. Still, he couldn't help noticing that she'd been looking better lately.

"I'm taking you kids out," said Aunt Ria. "You say where—I don't really know my way around yet."

"What about Dennis? I've got to pick him up."

"That's all been taken care of," her aunt reassured her.

"I know a great coffee shop," said Michael. He looked at Judith's aunt, and could easily imagine why Judith was so fond of her.

They sat down at a table by the window.

"Order whatever you like," said Aunt Ria. "I will, too."

A few minutes later, Judith and Michael were spooning up ice cream sundaes. Aunt Ria listened, smiling, as Michael told her about his swimming coach.

"I can't stay too long," he said, "or Mr. Rovers'll kill me! If you're even five minutes late, he goes crazy!"

He also told her about how he'd started biking to the day-care center with Judith, after she'd been attacked by a bunch of bullies.

"Does Mommy know about that?" asked Aunt Ria. Judith squirmed in her chair.

"Of course!" cried Michael. "She was covered with bruises, even her face. But we haven't seen those creeps since, right Judith?" he said proudly. "And if they ever try anything like that again, they'll have to fight me first!"

Michael wiped his mouth with the back of his hand, and got up to leave. "Well, thanks for the sundae, Mrs., uh—"

"Just call me Ria," she smiled.

"Thanks for the sundae, Ria," he squeaked, pumping her hand up and down.

"Hope to see you again sometime, Michael."

"Me too. See you tomorrow, Judith."

He hurried out the door, and they watched through the window as he jumped on his bike, waved, and rode off.

"Nice guy," remarked Aunt Ria. "Is he your boyfriend?"

Judith nodded. She fiddled with her napkin. "You won't tell Mommy, will you?"

"About Michael? That he's your boyfriend, you mean?"

Judith nodded again. Suddenly there was a dark shadow over the afternoon.

"Doesn't she know about him?"

"No."

"He's never been to your house?"

"He did come once, but Mommy wasn't very happy about it. She's always afraid I won't take good care of Dennis if there's somebody visiting."

"And do you ever go to his house?" asked Aunt Ria. She

saw Judith hesitating. "You can trust me, sweetie. I won't tell Mommy anything you don't want me to."

Judith looked up at her, relieved. "I go home with Michael every day for lunch. It's so much fun at his house. He lives with his aunt and uncle, because his mother's dead and his father lives in America and ..."

Aunt Ria listened, asking a question every now and again, and her amazement grew. Why was Judith keeping all this from her mother?

"Sounds like a wonderful family," she said when Judith was finished. "I can certainly imagine why you like going there so much."

Judith nodded enthusiastically.

"How did you meet Michael?"

"He's in my class. One time I had a flat tire, and ..." Judith plunged into another story. Now and then she stumbled over her words.

"He said I looked like Steffie, the girl who lived next door to him in America. She gave him her favorite bear, a koala bear from Australia. That's why he liked me, because I looked like Steffie. But now he likes me because I'm Judith. Just plain Judith." She stopped suddenly, as if she'd said more than she meant to.

Aunt Ria clasped her hands. "I like you because you're just plain Judith, too."

For a moment, Judith didn't know which way to look.

"Oh, Aunt Ria, I wish you could live with us forever," she said.

"I'm afraid Uncle Chris would put up a fuss." Aunt Ria smiled. "But I hope you'll come stay with us whenever you can. Of course, I've got to find a house first!"

Aunt Ria paid the bill and they walked outside arm in arm.

EIGHTEEN

WHEN AUNT RIA WENT AWAY, THE HOUSE SEEMED EMPTY. Judith missed her very much, especially in the evenings, but at night too. Some nights, Aunt Ria used to wake up when Judith's alarm clock went off, but instead of getting annoyed, she'd whisper to her in the darkness: kind words, words of encouragement. Judith's bed hadn't been wet once since the day she arrived.

Now the nights were lonely again. Each time Judith felt her way down the stairs and then back up to her room, she longed to hear the familiar creaking of the bed. Sometimes she even imagined she could hear her aunt's breathing, but it was only the wind.

Her mother was very irritable these days; the lines around her mouth grew sharper. Was it because of Aunt Ria's leaving, or because of Nico, who'd stopped coming around as much? Whenever he called to cancel a date, Judith had to be extra careful. She tried hard to stay out of her mother's way, but that only made things worse. "Quit sneaking around the house like that," Mommy snapped. "You're getting on my nerves."

Her mother also sounded her out about Aunt Ria.

"You probably thought I didn't notice the way you two were sitting around gossiping."

"We weren't gossiping, Mommy. Really."

"Then what *did* you talk about?"

"Oh, about school, and ..." She almost said Michael, but caught herself just in time. "And my teacher," she went on quickly. "His father's still in the hospital. And Aunt Ria talked a lot about Canada."

"She never talked about the past?"

Judith hesitated. "Sometimes."

"What do you mean, 'sometimes'?"

"Like ... you know ... she told me about when she was a little girl," Judith stammered.

Her mother eyed her suspiciously. "Did she say anything about Dicky?"

"Yes, that he fell through the ice, but I already knew that."

"And what else?"

"That I look like him." There was a tense silence; Judith avoided her mother's eyes.

"Is that it?"

"Yes."

"I'll bet," her mother sneered, but fortunately, she didn't ask any more questions.

A few days later, Judith was awakened by loud voices. She shot up in bed and listened, her heart pounding. She always left her bedroom door half-open at night, so she wouldn't make any noise when she went downstairs, and now she could hear every word. Her mother and Nico were having a fight.

"Give me back my money!" her mother screamed. "You've been robbing me for weeks!"

"Don't get so hysterical. You're the most paranoid person I've ever met. You always think everybody's out to get you!"

"I don't think *everybody's* out to get me, just *you*! You stole my money. Judith even saw you digging around in my bag!"

"You mean your daughter? The one you never have anything nice to say about? You've got to be kidding!" Nico jeered. "She probably pinched it herself!"

"Okay, then show me what you've got in your wallet."

"Why should I?" said Nico defiantly.

"Because this is the fourth time, since I met you, that there's money missing. First it was a hundred guilders, then fifty, last week twenty-five, and now I'm missing another fifty."

Her mother's voice was shrill with rage. "When I got home, there was a hundred fifty guilders in my wallet. I checked. Now there's only a hundred. There's only one person who could've stolen it, and that's you. Admit it!"

Nico laughed scornfully. "You wanna see fifty-guilder notes? Here, look, I've got three of 'em. But how're you going to prove that one of them is yours? Soon you'll be telling me I stole all three!"

There was a brief silence. Judith waited nervously to see what would happen.

"This is it!" her mother cried triumphantly. "I wrote my name on it, see? Here it is! I think I'll just keep the rest, too. That's letting you off easy!"

"Give me back that money, dammit!" shouted Nico.

"No way!"

Judith heard a lot of thumping and panting. Were they trying to hurt each other?

Dennis began to cry. Then there were loud, angry footsteps on the stairs, and the front door banged shut.

Judith's head throbbed. Her brother's crying grew louder; she heard her mother trying to calm him down. The light was on in the hallway, and a wide, yellowy-white streak fell into her room.

She thought of a few weeks earlier, when Mommy had accused her of stealing the money, and how furious she'd been when Judith had said it was Nico. She'd refused to believe her.

Dennis's crying stopped, the light was switched out in the hallway, and the house was silent once more.

The next morning not a word was said about the fight with Nico. Mommy's face was stony, her eyes swollen. Judith made herself as small as possible and did whatever she was told. One wrong move and her mother would explode, Judith was sure of it.

When she finally got outside, she breathed a sigh of relief. She quickly brought Dennis to the daycare center and then hurried on to school.

At lunch time, as she and Michael were cycling home to his house, he said, "Guess who called last night?"

"Who?"

"My dad."

"Did he call you from America?"

"No, he's still in Frankfurt."

"What did he want?"

"He just wanted to know how I was. I told him I'd been sick for a couple of days, and then he asked if he could stop by on his way back to America."

"What did you say?"

Michael stared straight ahead. "I said yes. Isn't that stupid?"

"Why is it stupid?"

"Because I'm afraid things'll be just like they used to be. In other words, lousy."

"But last time he was here—"

"I know, but still ..."

"So why didn't you say no?"

Michael shrugged. "Who knows," he said, sighing. "Maybe I'm still just too scared to say no to him."

"Or maybe you were hoping it would be like the last time."

Michael looked at her in surprise. "Yeah, I was," he admitted. "But now I really wish he wasn't coming. Every time I think about it, I get a cramp in my stomach."

"It'll probably all turn out fine," Judith reassured him, but even she knew it didn't sound very convincing. She could imagine how Michael must be feeling.

"That's easy for you to say," Michael muttered. "You haven't got a father."

Easy! thought Judith. If only he knew ...

That evening, as Judith was sitting and doing her homework, the phone rang. Her mother answered it.

"Excuse me?" she said. "Oh, Mr. Beekman! Hello! What can I do for you?"

Judith listened in, but she couldn't make any sense out of it. She began getting nervous. What did her teacher want? She didn't dare look at her mother, but she could tell by her sugary voice that there was trouble ahead.

"Oh, what a shame, I can't make it that day," her mother was saying. "I have to go to work. Can't we discuss it over the phone?"

Judith gulped. An invisible band tightened around her throat. Why would Mr. Beekman want to talk to her mother?

She heard her inventing excuses, and gathered that her teacher was trying to make an appointment, which her mother was trying to get out of. When that didn't work, she finally gave in.

"Okay, fine, next week ... No, I'm so sorry, this week is really impossible." Her voice remained friendly, but Judith knew better. Whenever her mother felt cornered, you had to watch out. Sure enough: no sooner had she hung up the phone than she began yelling, "What the hell was that all about? Why does your teacher want to talk to me?"

"I don't know," whispered Judith.

Her mother sprang up, grabbed Judith by the shoulders, and shook her roughly back and forth.

"You've been blabbing, haven't you? Telling all kinds of lies about me?"

Judith tried to dodge the blows, but it was no use.

"Maybe I should just tell your teacher what kind of person *you* are!"

All the pent-up rage of the last few days erupted on Judith's back, arms, and legs. Her mother pounded and kicked, flinging her on the ground and pulling her back up by the hair.

"Not my face, not my face," Judith moaned.

"Get out of here," her mother panted, "before I kill you!"

Judith stumbled up the stairs to her room.

Hours later, Judith heard soft, weary footsteps on the stairs. She lay as still as a statue. Her mother's silhouette appeared in the doorway. The footsteps approached her bed. She broke out in a sweat, her back stung, but she had to pretend to be asleep, or else ...

"Judith," her mother whispered hoarsely, "Judith ..."

She leaned over her. Judith felt the warmth of her breath against her cheek. Her temples throbbed. Even though her mother had never laid a hand on her when she was asleep, she expected, any minute now, to feel those iron fingers around her throat.

"Judith ..." she whispered again. It sounded like a plea.

Judith lay still and breathed as deeply and evenly as she could. But her heart was racing.

Her mother straightened up again, stood there for a moment, and then walked out of the room. As soon as Judith heard her footsteps on the stairs, she began to shake, an uncontrollable shivering, as if she had a live wire running through her. Even her teeth were chattering. She felt hot, then cold, then hot again; her pajamas stuck to her back.

Downstairs, she heard her mother switch off the light in the hallway. She was probably going to bed now.

The shivering went on for a while. Judith's back tingled; her arms and legs ached, too, and there was something wrong with her ankle. She'd twisted it when her mother threw her on the ground, and it hurt her every time she moved her leg.

Judith waited until the house was quiet. Then she carefully climbed out of bed and made her way downstairs, to the bathroom. When she got back to bed, she lay there, dry-eyed, staring into the darkness.

"I'm Judith," she whispered. "I'm Judith." She repeated her name over and over, as if she were trying to drum it into her own head.

NINETEEN

"WHAT'S WRONG WITH YOUR LEG?" MR. BEEKMAN ASKED THE next morning when Judith came limping into the classroom.

"Twisted my ankle," Judith mumbled. She quickly took her seat, hoping he wouldn't ask any more questions.

"How did *that* happen?" Diana wanted to know.

"I jumped off a wall, and I must've landed wrong," Judith told her.

"That was dumb. So now you'll have to miss gym again, right?"

"Yes."

"Too bad for you. We've got handball today."

"Yes, too bad," said Judith. She'd discovered that the best way to deal with Diana was to agree with everything she said. Then she usually left you alone. But not this time, unfortunately.

"There's always something wrong with you," Diana remarked. "One day you've got a headache, then it's the flu or a sprained ankle. I think you just don't like gym, and you make up all kinds of excuses to get out of it."

"Diana, would you let me know when you're finished, so we can begin?" said Mr. Beekman, and much to Judith's relief, she shut up.

But when it was time for gym and everyone went racing out the door, Diana shouted, "What a surprise! Judith has to miss gym again!"

Judith pretended not to hear, but she felt her cheeks burning. She stayed behind with her teacher, and when everyone was gone he asked, "How did you hurt your ankle?"

"I jumped off a wall, and I guess I just landed wrong," Judith lied again.

"That must've been very painful. Is it swollen?"

"A little."

"Have you wrapped a bandage around it?"

Judith shook her head.

"Let's have a look," said Mr. Beekman, walking over to her desk.

Judith held out her leg.

"You'll have to take off your shoe and sock," her teacher said, laughing. "I can't see through them!"

He waited patiently until Judith was ready, then examined her foot.

"Hmmm, it's pretty swollen. No wonder you're limping so badly. I'll go have a look in the first-aid kit and see if we've got any bandages. Okay?"

A few minutes later, he came back with the first-aid kit. He sat down opposite her, gently took hold of her foot, and rolled up her pant leg.

"What the—you're all covered with bruises!" he cried, looking down at her leg.

Judith turned pale with fear. She hadn't been expecting this.

In the silence that followed, Mr. Beekman rolled up her other pant leg. More bruises; some of them had already turned yellowish-green.

"How did this happen, Judith?" He looked at her gravely.

Judith blinked nervously. "It's ... It's ..." she whispered. "It's those boys."

"What boys?"

She shrugged.

"How many are there?"

"Three. Sometimes four."

"And they beat you up?"

She nodded vigorously.

Mr. Beekman took hold of her arms, one by one, and carefully rolled up her sleeves.

"Oh my God!" he said softly.

He went and stood behind her, and started to pull up her sweater.

"No!" Judith jumped up, forgetting all about her ankle. Her leg gave way, and she grabbed on to the edge of her desk. Her eyes were wide with fear.

"Does your mother know about this?" Mr. Beekman asked worriedly.

Confused, Judith nodded her head, then shook it.

"Yes or no?"

"Sometimes I tell her," said Judith, her lips trembling, "but sometimes I don't, because I don't want to get her all worried."

"I can imagine that," said her teacher. "But didn't your mother notice you were limping?"

"I told her I twisted my ankle." It came out in a whisper.

"And those bruises?"

"I didn't show her those." Judith stared unhappily at the floor.

"Does this happen often?"

She shrugged.

"Does it?" he asked her again.

"Only now and then."

"Tell me more about these boys. Do you know where they live?"

"No."

"Do they wait for you?"

Judith nodded.

"And then?"

"Then they start hitting and punching."

"Just like that? Right in the middle of the street?" asked Mr. Beekman, amazed.

"There's usually nobody else around."

"And why do they do it?"

"I don't know."

"Are these the same boys who used to attack you?"

"When?" Judith looked at him in confusion.

"When you were still at Margriet School. Didn't the same thing happen to you then?"

This caught her completely by surprise. How could he know that she'd used the same excuse at Margriet School?

"They're different boys," she finally answered.

Mr. Beekman looked at her closely, but Judith avoided his eyes.

"Has your mother ever reported this to the police?"

"Yes, I think so," whispered Judith.

"I phoned your mother last night to make an appointment to see her. I know you've really been doing your best in class, Judith, but you've been absent quite a lot, and I think she and I should talk about it."

"You won't tell her about those boys, will you?" Judith begged.

"Why not?"

"Because she'll just get worried all over again, and she has to work so hard, for me and my little brother." Judith tugged nervously at her sleeve.

Mr. Beekman was silent for a moment.

"Hey, don't look so sad," he said, brushing the hair out of her eyes. "Come on, I'll bandage your foot, but we'll have to make sure you can still get into your shoe. Otherwise you won't be able to go to Michael's house for lunch!"

"There," he said when he was finished. "Try walking around a bit, see how it feels."

Judith squeezed into her shoe and took a few careful steps.

"It feels much better," she said with a weak smile. "It hardly hurts at all anymore."

"Good," said her teacher. "But try to keep off that foot as much as possible. Why don't you stay here in the classroom? You can do some reading or get started on your homework. I'm just going down to get a cup of coffee."

She heard his footsteps fading away in the corridor and the vague hum of voices in the room next door. On her desk lay a pile of books and a blank sheet of paper. Before she knew it, she'd picked up a pencil and begun scribbling on the empty page, a confused tangle of jittery lines that grew larger, and larger, and larger.

That night Mr. Beekman told his wife what had happened.

"Something's going on with that child. A few weeks ago I spoke to a teacher at Margriet School, and she told me exactly the same story: Judith was often home sick, or there'd be something wrong with her and she'd have to miss gym. There was even a group of boys who used to beat her up on her way home from school."

"That *is* strange," his wife agreed.

"Fortunately, I've got an appointment to see her mother the day after tomorrow."

"You don't think she's being physically abused, do you?" his wife suddenly asked.

"Abused? You mean, by her mother?"

"Yes."

"The thought has crossed my mind. But I find it so hard to believe."

Abused ... He couldn't stop thinking about it for the rest of the evening.

"How's your ankle?" Mr. Beekman asked the next morning. He laid his hand on her shoulder and saw how she jumped at his touch. Ordinarily he might not even have noticed, but now he thought it was suspicious.

At recess, he asked Michael, "Would you mind helping me lug up some boxes?"

"No problem," said Michael.

They walked down to the storage room, and Mr. Beekman pointed out a couple of boxes. "Those have to go upstairs."

"No problem," Michael said again.

"Do you still bike home with Judith every day after school?" Mr. Beekman asked when they were back in the classroom.

"Yes, except Tuesdays, because then I've got practice at four o'clock."

"You two seem to get along very well together."

"Yeah, we do." Michael smiled shyly. "Judith's cool."

"You're right about that," said his teacher.

"It's a good thing she hasn't had any more trouble with those creeps," Michael blurted out.

"What creeps?"

"Well, a while back, she got beaten up by these kids on the street. When I saw her limping around yesterday, I was afraid maybe they'd started up all over again," Michael told him. "But she'd just sprained her ankle."

The teacher piled the boxes on top of each other in the

closet. So Judith hadn't told Michael she'd been attacked! Why was she keeping it a secret?

"Thank you, Michael," he said. "Go on outside. I don't want you to miss all of recess."

"That's okay, Mr. Beekman." He hesitated, and then said, "My father's here visiting us."

It was the first time Mr. Beekman had ever heard Michael talk about his father. "He lives in America, doesn't he?"

"Yes. He had to go to Frankfurt. Tomorrow morning he's flying back to America."

"Sounds like a busy man."

"And I might be going to America too," Michael told him, "for Easter vacation."

"Great!" said Mr. Beekman. "Some people have all the luck. How long has it been since you were there?"

"More than three years."

"That's a long time."

Michael nodded. "I, uh ... I didn't like it there very much," he admitted.

"A lot can change in three years. You're older now. It'll probably seem very different from when you were younger."

Michael nodded.

Mr. Beekman walked him to the door. "Next time your father comes, have him call me. Then I can tell him how proud I am of you." He tugged at Michael's hair.

Michael blushed. "Okay, Mr. Beekman," he said shyly, and ran out the door.

That same afternoon Mr. Beekman got a phone call from Judith's mother, canceling their appointment.

"I'm so sorry, but something's come up," she told him.

"Then we'll make a new appointment. Just say when."

"I'll call you," said Judith's mother.

But this time Mr. Beekman wasn't going to be put off. "I'd rather make the appointment now, if you don't mind. There's something I have to speak to you about, immediately."

There was a brief silence.

"It'll have to be next week, then."

They made another appointment, but Judith's mother never showed up.

"It completely slipped my mind," she apologized when Mr. Beekman phoned her. "What? Here? Oh no, I'm really sorry, I can't have you over today. I've got company. I can't make it next week either, and then it's Easter vacation. Time goes so quickly! But I'll call you right after Easter, I promise."

And before he could say another word, she'd hung up the phone.

TWENTY

MICHAEL FELT THE PLANE SLOWLY BEGINNING ITS DESCENT. Soon he'd have to buckle his seat belt, and in less than half an hour he'd be back at Schiphol Airport.

He gazed out the window. Way down below, puffy clouds drifted in a clear blue sky, like clouds in a picture book.

What a strange vacation it had been!

One morning he'd suddenly announced that he'd decided to accept his father's invitation to go to Washington for Easter.

Uncle Bob and Aunt Elly were amazed.

"Are you sure you want to go alone?" they'd asked him.

"I'm sure."

"But why all of a sudden?"

"If I wait too long, I'll probably lose my nerve," he'd told them. "Besides, I can always change my mind."

But he didn't. He got on the plane and went.

His father had picked him up at the airport.

"I'm so glad you've come," he said, and as they were walking to the car he asked, "Would you mind if we stayed at Helen's house while you're here?" Michael shook his head, but deep down he dreaded seeing her again.

His father didn't say much during the drive, but Michael noticed that he glanced at him every now and again.

"You seem to have grown even taller these past few weeks," he said.

"It's possible." Michael didn't say that he thought his father was getting shorter; they were nearly the same height.

"You'll probably end up taller than I am."

"I wouldn't be surprised," said Michael. His father smiled.

It was a shock seeing Helen's house again. Some things were so clearly etched in his memory, the recognition was almost painful.

First of all, Helen: unchanged, perhaps a bit smaller and wirier than he'd remembered, but that was probably because he was taller.

She seemed genuinely happy to see him again. She put her hands on his shoulders and looked him over, from head to toe, with her green, gold-flecked eyes.

"Michael ..." Once again she didn't say Mike but Michael, with an American accent. "I can't believe how much you've grown. And look at those muscles! Your father ought to follow your example."

Then they all walked into the kitchen, which hadn't changed either. He looked out at the garden.

"Yes, the tree's still there," said Helen, following his gaze. "Last year we picked baskets full of apples. We had enough for the whole neighborhood!"

She puttered about at the stove, making tea with the same ease he remembered from years ago, and she spoke to him as if he were an old friend. But *wasn't* he an old friend, even though they'd only met once? He'd never forgotten her. Nor had she forgotten him, as she admitted several days later, when they were drinking Coke in a nearby drugstore.

"I can still remember what you were wearing: an expensive blue jacket, a red T-shirt, and jeans ... and you looked frighteningly lonely."

I was, thought Michael, but he said nothing.

"I thought a lot about you after that, and about your father. He didn't even notice me when he came to pick you up. He must've been going out of his mind that night you were gone, but I'll bet he never let it show. I've never met anyone who can hide his feelings as well as your father. Fortunately, it's getting better."

"He has changed," said Michael carefully.

"That man works too hard." Helen shook her head. "He hardly ever has time to relax. So every now and then I drag him along to a play or a movie—he's always surprised at how much fun it can be! And we've always got plenty to talk about ..."

Helen played with her empty glass.

"Your father talks a lot about you."

Complains, you mean, thought Michael, staring straight ahead.

"He's often said that he hopes he'll get a second chance."

"Second chance?" Michael raised his eyebrows.

"To be your dad. That's why I'm so glad you came."

"As long as he doesn't think I'm coming back here to live!" he burst out.

"He doesn't," said Helen calmly. "Would you like some more soda?"

"Yes, please," Michael mumbled.

Helen ordered two more Cokes and then changed the subject.

One afternoon they all went to the swimming pool.

"You're a real champ!" Helen shouted enthusiastically when she saw him swimming.

A champ ... Michael felt his confidence growing, and tried his best to make a good time—and he *did*! Glowing with pride, he climbed out of the pool and flopped down next to Helen. They sat and watched his father, who was struggling to improve his breaststroke.

"Sometimes you remind me so much of your dad," Helen suddenly remarked.

"Me? I'm not at all like him!"

"Oh, yes, you are. You can be just as fanatic. Your swimming, for instance."

"You're not gonna tell me I swim like that!" cried Michael, pointing indignantly at his father. "Look at that breaststroke. It's pathetic!"

Helen laughed. "I wasn't comparing your swimming ability, I meant the way you both go about doing things. You swim with the same dedication and determination as your father when he's arguing a case."

"That's totally different."

"You think so?"

"Yeah, you've got to be really brilliant to argue a case ..."

"And what about you?" Helen flared up. "What you've managed to achieve in the water—don't you think that's brilliant too?"

"You don't need brains for that."

"You *do* need brains for that!" she burst out. "And perseverance. Talent alone isn't enough. You know, Michael, you can go far with swimming. Very far."

Michael was silent. He felt himself growing warm. "I'm training really hard at the moment. My coach wants me to join the swimming team."

"Yes, your father told me."

"But I'm still pretty hopeless at school," he admitted with a crooked grin.

"Do you think you'll pass this year?"

"Yeah, probably. But I'm not expecting too many *A*'s or *B*'s."

"That's not important. Your father'll never be a swimming champion, either. He should just be glad he doesn't sink!" She laughed, pushed Michael into the water, and dove in after him.

"Would all passengers please fasten their seat belts? We're about to land."

Michael jumped at the sound of the flight attendant's voice and quickly buckled his belt. They were flying straight through the clouds now; the plane rocked back and forth.

He had so much to tell everyone! Especially about the day before yesterday. His father had come home with a very mysterious expression on his face.

"We're going out tonight," he'd said.

"Where?" Helen and Michael had both asked at the same time.

"You'll have to wait and see."

"Brace yourself, Michael. It's probably something cultural. So, Dirk, what should I wear?"

"Wear?"

"You heard me," said Helen. "Not that you'll notice. You know, Michael, a couple of weeks ago we were going out ... I was walking around the house in my pajamas, and I thought: okay, time for a little test. I put on my shoes, grabbed my bag and said, 'Ready?' And I swear, your father would've walked right out the door with me dressed like that, if I hadn't said anything. I asked him, 'How do I look?' He peered down at me through those old-fashioned glasses of his and said, 'You look fine.'"

"You did." His father grinned. "Besides, those pajamas look exactly like a track suit. There's nothing wrong with wearing them outside."

"A track suit! I paid a fortune for those pajamas, they're real silk! You're hopeless," she said, laughing. "Now just tell me, what should I wear?"

"Something casual," suggested Michael's father. "How about a pair of pajamas?"

Helen flung a pillow at his head, which he dodged, with surprising agility, and flung right back.

First they'd had dinner at an Italian restaurant, and after that they'd gone to a basketball game. Michael could hardly believe his eyes when they were standing outside the enormous gymnasium. The Harlem Globetrotters! Even Helen was excited.

"How in the world did you get tickets?" she asked Michael's father. "*I've* never been able to pull that off."

"Oh, I've got a few connections in the sports world," he teased, "now that I'm a sportsman myself!"

It was an unforgettable game. The players, as usual, put on a real show. Even Michael's father enjoyed himself, and when it was over, they all went out for ice cream. They ate and laughed and talked about the game. His father knew more about basketball than Michael had expected.

"How do you know all that?" he asked curiously.

"Well ... As it happens, I've got a son who plays basketball, so every once in a while I buy myself a sports weekly."

"Why didn't you tell me?" he said happily. "I hope you've saved them all. Then I can read them, too."

And he had saved them, every one! That was just like his father. Michael had packed the whole stack in his suitcase. They were in English, which was a real challenge for him, but it was worth the effort.

Michael looked out the window. They were skimming over

the flat, green land stretching all the way to the horizon, criss-crossed with canals and dotted with red-roofed farmhouses. The sky had turned gray, and it was drizzling, but he didn't care. The runway came into view ...

Michael had a fluttery feeling in his stomach. He couldn't wait to see everyone. He'd need at least a day to tell them all about his trip. He especially couldn't wait to see Judith. He'd sent her a postcard and bought her a gift. Would she think it was too babyish? No, not Judith, he thought. Other people might, but not Judith.

TWENTY - ONE

MICHAEL WENT WHIZZING AROUND THE BEND. HE WAS ON HIS way to Judith's, and nearly burst with impatience at every red light. He still hadn't gotten over his disappointment that Judith's seat in class had been empty all day.

The day before, when he'd arrived home from America, Aunt Elly had baked a cake and decorated the living room with streamers. It was like a party! Everyone plied him with questions, and he tried to answer them all. The jet lag didn't hit him until several hours later, and then he'd almost fallen asleep in his chair. Yet tired as he was, he'd tried phoning Judith to see if she'd gotten his card, but nobody answered.

Michael pedaled like crazy. Two more streets, and he was there. When he rang her bell, he noticed the curtain moving in the first-floor window and caught a glimpse of a pale face.

Michael waited, but no one appeared. Once again he rang the bell, longer this time. Still no answer. He took a few steps back and peered up at the windows on the second floor. No sign of life.

The curtain in the first-floor window moved again. Was it just his imagination? No, the woman was beckoning to him. She seemed to have trouble making the gesture, as if her fingers were cramped. Michael went and stood at her door, which was next to Judith's.

Here, too, he had to wait, but after a while he heard slow, shuffling footsteps.

"What can I do for you?" asked the man standing opposite him.

"Let the boy in," came a voice from inside the house.

The man hesitated. "Are you here to see my wife?" he asked.

"Yes, sir."

"Are you going to let that boy in or aren't you?" The voice was brusque.

Moments later, Michael was standing in a stuffy, dark living room. Sitting at the window, with a plaid blanket over her legs, was the woman who had beckoned to him. He noticed that her hands were misshapen, her face deeply lined. She made no attempt to be friendly.

"I saw you ringing the bell next door."

"Yes, ma'am."

"They're gone."

Michael was stunned. This was the very last thing he'd expected.

"Gone?"

"We shouldn't get involved, Trude," her husband warned, but the woman paid no attention.

"Did you know those people?"

"Yes ... no ... uh, I mean, I only knew Judith. She was in my class."

"You've been here before, haven't you?"

Michael nodded. He was having a hard time absorbing the news he'd just heard. Judith gone ... But maybe he'd misunderstood, maybe they'd only gone on vacation!

"Do you know when they're coming back?"

The woman gave a scornful laugh.

"Coming back? They're never coming back. They've moved! In one of those VW buses. They just packed everything up and drove off."

"Did they ... did they leave their address?"

"Nothing. Didn't even say good-bye. That poor child did wave to me, though, the little girl ... You say she was in your class?"

Michael nodded dejectedly. Why hadn't Judith told him they were moving?

"Did she ever say anything to you?"

"Trude," her husband warned, "we shouldn't get—"

"Mind your own business," his wife snapped.

"Well, did she?" She gave Michael a scrutinizing look.

"What do you mean?"

"About her being beaten?"

"Trude!"

"Would you shut up and let me talk to the boy!" she cried impatiently, and turned back to Michael. "Did you know she used to get beat up all the time?"

"I know she got attacked once. That's why I biked home with her after school. But I never actually saw the boys who did it."

"Boys? What boys?"

"The ones who beat her up so badly."

"Boys!" Once again, that scornful laugh. "She told you they were boys? It was her own mother!"

Michael stared at her in amazement. The blood rushed to his head, and he felt himself growing dizzy in that cramped, overheated room.

"Her mother?"

"Bet that comes as a surprise, doesn't it? That woman beat the living daylights out of her. You could sometimes hear her screaming from here!"

"But ... but ..." stuttered Michael, "why didn't you do anything about it?"

"You shouldn't interfere in other people's business," muttered the old man.

"*That's* why!" the woman burst out. "Every time I said we had to help the poor child, my husband said it was none of our business."

"It's *not* our business. The world is full of problems. You can't solve them all. Anyway, nobody asked you to get involved."

But Michael had stopped listening. He was thinking of the bruises, the welts on her back. Her mother! Why had Judith kept it from him, even lied about it? He was her boyfriend, wasn't he?

"What was that little girl's name again?" asked the woman.

"Judith," mumbled Michael. He had to get out of there; he could hardly breathe.

"I've gotta go." He turned around and fled from the room.

Outside, he took a deep breath, then jumped on his bike and rode off, without looking back once.

His legs moved automatically, and after a while he noticed he was going the wrong way. In a daze, he turned around and cycled home. When he got there, he realized that his cheeks were wet. Angrily, he wiped them dry with his jacket sleeve. He slammed his bike against the shed, ran straight up to his room, and threw himself down on the bed.

After a while, there was a soft knock on his door, and moments later he heard Aunt Elly's voice, right by his ear. "Michael?"

He was lying on his stomach, his head buried in the pillow.

He felt a hand on his hair, on his shoulder. "What's the matter?"

Michael answered her with a muffled sob. Aunt Elly said nothing, just sat there stroking his hair.

"Is it your father?" she asked, when several minutes had passed.

Michael shook his head vehemently and buried it deeper into the pillow.

"Did something happen at school?"

"No," he sniffed.

Aunt Elly stood up, went to the dresser, and got out a handkerchief. "Here, honey."

Michael blew his nose loudly.

"Judith's g-gone," he stammered out. "She's moved away."

"Oh, no ..." said Aunt Elly. "Where to?"

"I don't know. And that's not all ... Her mother ... her mother beats her. I heard it from the lady who lives downstairs from them."

Aunt Elly stared at him in disbelief.

"Judith told me some boys had beaten her up." Michael's voice broke. "Remember? That time I went to see her. She was bruised all over, even her back. The lady downstairs said she used to hear her screaming."

"Oh, my God," whispered Aunt Elly, horrified. "Why didn't the woman try to stop it, if she knew what was going on?"

"She's in a wheelchair. And her husband kept telling her it was none of their business."

Aunt Elly shook her head. "I don't understand ... How could I not have noticed? I did think Judith looked kind of unhealthy sometimes, but some kids are just naturally pale. And she was so quiet—though lately, she'd started opening up a bit."

"I always thought it was weird that she wouldn't let me visit her," Michael admitted. "She always had some excuse. She once told me that her mother didn't know she came here for lunch. It was a secret."

"That poor child ..."

"But why didn't she say anything? I thought I was her friend." Michael stared down at the floor. Aunt Elly could tell by his voice how hurt he was.

"I suppose it's the kind of thing you don't dare tell anybody about. Especially if it's your own mother. I think I'd keep it a secret, too."

"And she did so much to help her mother out!" cried Michael. "She picked up her brother every day, took care of him, helped around the house, and her mother never let her go anywhere!"

Aunt Elly shook her head again. "If only we could find out where she lived."

"Maybe my teacher knows," said Michael hopefully. "I'll ask him first thing tomorrow morning."

The next day Michael hurried to school. He'd lain awake half the night, worrying about Judith. He just had to find a way to get her address!

As he was walking down the corridor, he suddenly felt a hand on his shoulder. "Can I speak to you at recess?" asked his teacher.

"Sure, Mr. Beekman." Great, he thought. Now he could ask him about Judith.

But his teacher beat him to it. No sooner had the last pupils left the classroom than he asked, "Do you know where Judith is?"

"I was just going to ask you the same thing," said Michael. "I know she's moved, but I don't know where to."

A worried wrinkle appeared in Mr. Beekman's forehead.

"Had she ever mentioned anything to you about moving?"

"No. I went over to see her yesterday, but nobody answered the door. One of her neighbors told me they'd left."

The teacher looked at him anxiously and began pacing up and down. "Michael, I'm afraid there may be something wrong with Judith."

"There *is* something wrong," Michael blurted out. His voice broke. "She ... she gets beaten!"

The teacher stopped dead. "By whom?"

"By her mother."

"Her mother? How long have you known that?"

"Only since yesterday." Michael swallowed hard. "I tried calling Judith on the phone, but no one answered. So I rode over to her house ..." His voice faltered as he told his teacher what he'd heard from Judith's neighbor.

Mr. Beekman sat down at his desk and shook his head in dismay. "A while ago, I noticed that Judith's arm was all bruised. She told me she'd crashed into a cabinet when she was playing with her brother. But just before Easter, she sprained her ankle—remember?"

Michael nodded. Judith had told him she'd jumped off a wall and landed wrong.

"When I was bandaging her ankle, I found bruises on her legs, and both arms this time. She said she'd been attacked by a group of boys. I happen to know that that's the same excuse she used at her old school, so this has obviously been going on for quite a while. Did you suspect anything at all?"

"Only that one time ..." said Michael hesitantly, "when I went to visit Judith. You remember, you gave me a bag of licorice for her, because she was sick again. When I got there, she had a bruise on her cheek, and more bruises all over her back ... But I really believed her when she said it was the boys who'd done it."

Michael stared miserably at the floor, and kicked his foot against the table leg.

Mr. Beekman stood up and laid his hand on Michael's shoulder. "It must've been terrible for her, Michael, if she couldn't even tell you."

Michael had a burning feeling in his throat.

"Do you know her mother?" asked his teacher.

"I only met her once. She didn't even know who I was, and she also didn't know anything about Judith coming home with me for lunch."

The teacher shook his head. "Judith needs help, and so does her mother, before things get out of hand. But how are we going to find out her address? All we got was a message that they'd moved, nothing more."

"You could try calling all the schools in town," suggested Michael.

"I'll do that," his teacher promised. "Today. Does Judith have any relatives?"

"Yes, an aunt, but I don't know her address either." He thought for a while. "The daycare center!" he suddenly cried. "Sophie works there. Maybe she can help us."

"Okay, you go down to the daycare center, and I'll call the schools. As soon as we find out anything, we'll let each other know. Is it a deal?"

Michael nodded eagerly.

They heard the bell; recess was over.

TWENTY - TWO

THE NEXT MORNING MR. BEEKMAN TOOK MICHAEL ASIDE.

"I've called all the schools, but she's not enrolled at any of them. I'm afraid Judith must've moved to another city."

"Sophie couldn't help me either," Michael told him. "They didn't leave any address behind at the daycare center."

But that afternoon, when he and his family were just sitting down to lunch, the phone rang.

"Would you get it?" asked Aunt Elly.

Michael walked into the hallway and picked up the receiver. "Hello?"

There was a silence on the other end of the line.

"Hello?" he repeated. "Who is this?"

"It's Judith," said a soft voice.

"Judith!" His voice broke with excitement. "Judith, where are you?"

"We moved."

"I know, but where are you living?"

A hesitant pause. "In Leiden. How was your trip?"

"I'll tell you all about it when I see you, because I really *have* to see you. I bought you a present. What's your address?"

Judith didn't answer that. "I'm calling from a phone booth," she said hurriedly. "I haven't got any more money, but I—"

There was a click, and they were cut off.

Michael stood there, dumfounded, staring at the receiver. He hung up and waited. Would she call him back?

After a while, Aunt Elly came in to see if anything was wrong.

"Judith?" she guessed immediately.

Michael nodded.

"She's living in Leiden, but before she could tell me where, we got cut off. She was calling from a phone booth."

"I'm sure she'll call you back," said Aunt Elly gently.

But she didn't.

—

Judith's hand shook as she hung up the phone. Michael's familiar voice had roused such a desperate longing in her, it made her dizzy. She'd been unable to resist the urge to call him, even though she knew she couldn't see him anymore, now that they'd moved.

"Hey, are you planning to spend all day in there?" A boy of about sixteen jerked open the door of the telephone booth.

Judith hurried out and grabbed her bike.

It was Market Day in Leiden. People were jostling each other in front of the stalls and milling about in the streets. Judith wormed her way through the crowds, then jumped on her bike and rode home, to the narrow side-street where her mother had rented an apartment.

Three weeks before, on the first day of Easter vacation, her mother had suddenly announced that they were moving.

"Where are we going?" she'd stammered.

"Leiden."

"Do I ... do I have to leave school?" She couldn't hide the fear in her voice.

"Of course you do. Did you think I was going to let you travel back and forth to the Hague every day? I'm just glad to be rid of that nosy teacher of yours. Who does he think he is, nagging me about making an appointment? If I have something to tell him, I'll call him myself."

Judith hadn't dared ask her any more about it. Nor did she even get the chance; her mother put her straight to work packing boxes.

The last night in her attic room, she'd lain her bed, tossing and turning. She thought of Michael, whom she'd never see again. Aunt Elly, either. There was a hard, dry lump in her throat, and she had trouble swallowing. She stared into the darkness, and finally, after what seemed like hours, she fell into a restless sleep.

Michael boarded the train to Leiden.

Once they knew that Judith was living in Leiden, it didn't

take Mr. Beekman long to find out what school she was going to, and where she lived.

"I better wait for her at school," Michael had said. "If I go to her house and her mother's there, I haven't got a chance."

"I suppose that means I'll have to give you the afternoon off?"

"Sorry, Mr. Beekman, I can't think of any other way."

"Okay," his teacher had said, laughing, "but just this once."

The train began moving; it glided slowly out of Central Station. Michael put the plastic bag next to him on the seat. Inside was the present he'd bought for Judith in America. Would she be glad to see him again? He was slightly nervous and had a funny feeling in his stomach. Now that the time had come, he wasn't even sure what he was going to say to her.

Before he knew it, they were pulling into Leiden. He lifted his bicycle off the train. There was a map in his pocket, but he already knew which route to take.

Michael walked out of the station, jumped on his bike, and sped off.

Judith's school was in a new suburb, with very little greenery. It was an L-shaped building with a playground in front. The bicycle rack must be around the back, thought Michael. Which class was Judith in, and what should he do if she wasn't at school today? Should he go to her house after all?

He was much too early, and had to wait. He shifted restlessly from one leg to the other. When the bell finally rang, he jumped, and his heart started pounding.

The children piled out: first the very youngest, then the rest. The air was filled with their cries. The oldest children came out the back entrance, wheeling their bikes. Judith wasn't among them.

He stood there anxiously, waiting and watching, and suddenly he saw her. She was walking her bike with the other children, but they weren't paying her the least bit of attention. She looks so small, thought Michael. She had her head bowed, her eyes on the ground, and she probably would've walked right past him if Michael hadn't called out her name.

She stopped short and looked up. The expression on her face changed from one of disbelief to one of happiness. A boy walking behind her bumped into her, but she didn't even notice.

"Hi," was all Michael could think of saying.

"Hi," said Judith.

"Which way are you going?" asked Michael.

"That way." Judith was about to get on her bike.

"Do you feel like a Coke or something?" asked Michael.

He saw her hesitate. "I ... uh ... I don't really have much time."

"Do you have to pick up Dennis?"

"No. Dennis is with my mother ... I mean, she works at an office that has its own daycare center." Judith thought of all the shopping she had to do, and ...

"Then we've got plenty of time to get something to drink," Michael decided.

"Okay," said Judith softly. She still couldn't believe he was here.

"How did you know I went to this school?"

"Mr. Beekman told me. When I told him you were living in Leiden, he phoned a couple of schools here until he found the right one. By the way, he says hello."

Judith smiled.

It took them a while to find a coffee shop that wasn't too crowded. Michael led her over to a table in the corner.

"What would you like to drink?"

"Chocolate milk," said Judith.

A waitress came and took their orders. When she was gone, Michael said, "I've got something for you." He put the plastic bag on the table.

"For me?" Judith blushed. She opened the bag and peeked inside.

"Ohhh ..." She reached in and took out a small brown teddy bear. When she looked up at Michael, her eyes were filled with tears.

"Do you like him?"

Judith swallowed hard, and all she could do was nod.

The waitress brought their drinks. "What a cute little bear," she said, smiling.

"Yeah, I thought so, too," said Michael. "That's why I bought it."

Judith wiped her eyes with the back of her hand. Why did she have to start blubbering? What would Michael think?

Neither of them said a word.

"Did you buy him in America?" Judith asked after a while.

"Yeah. Helen—that's my dad's girlfriend—Helen and I went to this gigantic toy store, and there he was, sitting in the window."

"Did he make you think of Steffie?"

"No, he made me think of you. He just looked s-so ..." Michael began stuttering. "W-what I mean is, I liked him right away. And you? You don't think he's too babyish?"

Judith shook her head vehemently. "I think he's great. Really. This is the best present I ever had." She stroked the bear's head.

The feeling of closeness was back between them.

"So ... how was it in America?" she asked carefully.

"A lot better than I expected," Michael admitted. "I wasn't looking forward to it, but Helen's a nice lady, we got along really well, and my father ... my father's changed. You know something, he's a pretty nice guy!"

He was silent for a moment, and then asked, "Why didn't you tell me you were moving to Leiden?"

"I didn't know about it yet. My mother suddenly got a new job, and then it all went so quickly."

"But why didn't you at least leave an address?"

Judith looked down and fiddled with one of the bear's ears.

"Or were you not allowed to?"

"I was never going to see you again anyway," Judith mumbled, "so there was no point leaving my address."

Michael mustered up his courage, and blurted out, "Judith, I know about your mother."

Her consternation was so great, she nearly knocked over her chocolate milk.

He leaned toward her. "That afternoon when I came to visit you ... when you told me those boys had beaten you up?"

Judith was breathing quickly, like someone who felt cornered.

"Why didn't you tell me the truth? I'm your friend, aren't I?" He sounded hurt.

She nodded.

"I saw all those bruises, on your face and on your back. And the time you sprained your ankle—did your mother do that too?"

Judith didn't answer that. "How ... how did you find out?" she asked brokenly, staring straight ahead.

"From your downstairs neighbor, that old lady who's always sitting at the window. I rang your doorbell, but nobody answered. Then she started waving to me to come over. She told me ... she told me she used to hear you screaming."

Judith clasped the bear to her chest, as if she were seeking comfort.

"Why does your mother beat you?"

"I don't know," she said tonelessly.

"Does she beat Dennis, too?"

"No, not Dennis."

"So why you?"

Judith shrugged her shoulders.

"Is that why you had to skip gym all the time? Is that why you were always sick?"

She nodded.

"But why do you let her do it?" Michael burst out.

Judith turned to him with a blank expression on her face.

"If you don't do anything, she'll keep on beating you. You've got to do something!"

Was any of this getting through to her?

"You've got to tell somebody. It's not normal for a mother to beat her child. It's just not normal!"

Slowly, Judith seemed to awaken from a kind of trance.

"How long has she been doing this?"

She looked away again. "As long as I can remember."

"Even when you were little?"

"Yes."

"But why, *why*?"

"I don't know, I really don't know." Judith plucked nervously at the bear's fur. "Maybe because I ... because I look like Dicky."

"Dicky? Who's Dicky?"

"My mother's brother. He died when he was nine or ten. He fell through the ice."

"So did she hate his guts or something?"

"No, I don't think so, I don't kn-know ..." Judith stammered, "but her mother, my grandmother, blamed the accident on her. He wanted to go skating, and my mother was supposed to watch him. That's when he fell through the ice. My Aunt Ria told me all about it. After Dicky died, Grandma didn't want to have anything more to do with my mother. She acted like Mommy didn't even exist."

"But you can't help it if you look like Dicky!" Michael cried indignantly.

Judith was still fiddling with the bear. Hesitantly, she said, "You liked me because I looked like Steffie. But what if Steffie had been a horrible person?"

"I would've liked you anyway," said Michael. "Because you're Judith, and ... well ... I really thought it was terrible when you moved, and I really miss you a lot."

"I miss you, too," admitted Judith.

There was a silence.

"You've got to do something," Michael insisted.

"But what?" She sounded helpless.

"Aunt Elly said you can always come live with us. We'll help you. She even offered to talk to your mother, or Aunt Ria."

Judith looked at him in terror. "Does Aunt Elly know too?"

"Yes."

"Who else?" Her lips began trembling.

"Mr. Beekman."

"Mommy'll think I've told everyone," she gasped. "She'll beat me to death if she finds out ..."

"She'll probably beat you to death anyway!" said Michael.

Judith was silent.

"Yes," she said, after a while. "You're right."

TWENTY - THREE

JUDITH CYCLED HOME. BECAUSE OF MICHAEL, SHE'D COMPLETELY forgotten about the time. Seeing him again so unexpectedly had confused her at first, especially when he told her he knew everything. But later on, it had been a great relief. She'd finally been able to tell him the truth: about the bag, about how her mother had suspected her of stealing the money ... Once she got started there was no stopping her; she talked on and on, and Michael listened in amazement.

"Why didn't you tell me all this before?" he asked.

"I *couldn't*. I really couldn't, Michael. And besides, I thought it was normal. Well, not exactly normal, but ... it's never been any other way. Sometimes things'll be going along fine, and Mommy doesn't beat me, and then all of a sudden everything goes wrong."

"Do you know why?"

Judith thought for a moment. "Sometimes I do—for instance, if something's happened at the office, but a lot of the time I don't. Usually I can tell it's coming, though, by the sound of her footsteps, or the way she looks at me, the way she moves. Then I have to be extra careful, but that only makes me more nervous, and then I can't do anything right."

"Don't you hate your mother for the way she treats you?" asked Michael.

Judith shrugged sadly. "I think I hate myself even more," she confessed, "because I'm so scared. I'm always just waiting for it to happen. And the waiting is the horrible part."

"If you go on waiting, your mother'll go on beating you."

His words had stuck in her mind.

"You've got to do something," he'd urged her again. "You can't keep this a secret. And we'll help you, I promise."

Judith arrived at her house, all out of breath. To her horror, she saw her mother's car parked outside the door. Was it that late already? She hadn't even done the shopping yet! And the teddy bear—her mother mustn't see him, no matter what.

He was too big to fit in her school bag. And there were no sheds around here that she could hide him in. Suddenly she had an idea: she'd take off her jacket and wrap him up in it.

She fumbled nervously with the key, then wheeled her bike into the narrow hallway. She climbed the stairs, her knees like jelly. At the top of the stairs, a door opened.

"Where have you been?"

Trouble, thought Judith. Halfway up the stairs she stopped, and hesitated. Only later did she realize that she should've turned around and ran.

Her mother stormed down the stairs and dragged her up by the hair. The pain was so intense that the screams stuck in her throat.

"Where were you!" her mother yelled, shaking her back and forth. "And where are the groceries?" She drove her into a corner, kicking and punching.

Judith couldn't dodge the blows; the hallway was too narrow. She tried desperately to shield her head. Her jacket fell to the ground, but she was still clutching the plastic bag with the bear inside.

Suddenly her mother stopped. "What've you got there?" she panted, snatching away the bag.

Judith's head was reeling. She watched, in a daze, as her mother pulled out the teddy bear.

"What the hell is this?"

"A present," Judith whispered faintly.

"Who gave it to you?"

She didn't answer.

"You bought it with the grocery money!" screamed her mother.

"No, no, Mommy, really!" cried Judith, terrified. "It was—"

"Then where's the wallet?"

"In the drawer!" Judith wailed.

"Show me!"

Her mother shoved her into the living room. Judith couldn't think straight. She didn't know where the wallet was. She stumbled over to the chest and pulled open a drawer. Everything swam before her eyes. She rummaged frantically among papers, boxes, and pens. Different drawer.

"M-maybe it's in the kitchen," she stammered. Her mother dragged her into the kitchen, and Judith pulled open the drawer where her mother kept the knives. Her mind was a total blank. "I don't ... I don't remember."

Her mother's hand came down hard against her cheek. How many blows followed, she didn't know. She was slammed against the counter, and felt something warm dripping from her nose.

"You bought that bear!" her mother hissed, grabbing a bread knife out of the drawer.

Judith gasped. "No, Mommy ... not the bear! Not the bear!" she shrieked.

She watched as her mother plunged the knife into the bear, four, five times, ripping it to shreds. Then she raised her arm again and started coming toward her. Judith froze, the knife flashed, and suddenly her mother lowered her hand.

She stared at Judith, panting, her face contorted with pain. "What am I doing? My God, what am I doing?"

She dropped the knife and buried her face in her hands.

Only then did Judith see Dennis standing in the doorway, his eyes wide with fear.

Trembling, Judith dabbed at her face with cold water. Her lip was already starting to swell; her left eye was half-shut.

My bear's gone ...

Something's wrong with my ribs, she thought. It hurt when she breathed. She'd wet her pants, too.

My bear's gone ...

Judith carefully got undressed, turned on the shower, and let the water stream down over her body.

My bear's gone ...

She began shaking violently, as if she were cold. And she *was* cold, cold as ice. Even the hot water felt cold.

My bear's gone ... My bear's gone ...

The rest of the evening passed like an old, familiar movie. The wallet was found, lying on a shelf. It was too late to go shopping, so her mother went out to get French fries, which Judith usually loved, but now they made her sick to her stomach. Still, she didn't refuse; she was afraid of another explosion.

Her mother told her that Uncle Ben, "that bastard," had phoned her at the office to let her know he wanted to see more of Dennis.

"First he couldn't give a damn about his own son, and all of a sudden he's father-of-the-year! But I'm not putting up with it," she rattled on excitedly. "He's never getting Dennis, that's for sure."

Judith listened, her temples throbbing. After supper she escaped to her room: a tiny cubicle, just big enough for a bed.

"It's only temporary," Mommy had said. "I'm looking for a bigger place."

She lay awake for hours, her head spinning.

You've got to do something ... You've got to do something ... Michael's words kept running through her mind.

She thought again and again of the moment when her mother plunged the knife into the bear and tore it apart. Her gift from Michael ...

Tears stung her eyes.

Judith carefully turned over. She was still having trouble breathing; she must've hurt her ribs when Mommy slammed her against the counter.

If I stay here, Mommy will tear me apart, too, thought Judith, just like my bear.

Once again, she heard Michael's voice, "You've got to do something ..."

"I'll call school and tell them you're not feeling well, and that you're staying home for a few days," her mother said the next morning.

Judith nodded. She didn't look at her.

As she was helping Dennis into his jacket, she whispered softly, "Good-bye, dear, dear Dennis," and kissed him. Her lips stung.

She heard her mother starting the car. The engine turned

over, once, twice. The third time, it caught. She drove down the street; the sound died away.

Judith cleared the table and washed the dishes. Just as she was about to throw something in the trash can, she saw the teddy bear, lying under a pile of French fries. She stood there looking at him, then got out a plastic bag, put him in it, and tied it closed.

After that, she got dressed and combed her hair.

She hunted through a closet for the overnight bag, found it, and stuffed it with clothes. She didn't take the red sweater. The plastic bag with the bear inside went on top, along with a picture of Dennis and her alarm clock.

She looked around the room, saw one of Dennis's cars lying under a chair, and put it back in his toy box.

Then she put on her jacket and walked down the stairs. She left her bike behind.

The bus stop was two blocks away. She had to walk very slowly because her ribs hurt, especially now that she was carrying the heavy bag. Judith could feel people staring at her. She knew her lip was swollen, and that she had a black eye. In a couple of days it would turn greenish-yellow.

As she boarded the bus to the train station, the driver asked, "Been in a fight, kid? A little thing like you?"

Judith tried to laugh, but it was more of a crooked grin. She found a seat at the back and stared fixedly out the window.

"Leiden Central!" The driver's voice made her jump. She hurriedly grabbed her bag—ow, her ribs!—and lugged it off the bus.

"One-way ticket to the Hague," she said to the girl behind the window.

ALSO BY ANKE DE VRIES

My Elephant Can Do Almost Anything

Piggy's Birthday Dream

ANKE DE VRIES is an award-winning Dutch author. She is the mother of three children and lives part time in The Hague and part time in La-Bégude-de-Mazenc, France.

STACEY KNECHT won the James F. Holmes Translation award for Lieve Joris' *Back to the Congo*. She lives in Zwolle, the Netherlands.